THE BOOK
OF
MANCHESTER

EDITED BY
DAVID SUE

'Abduction' was first published in *Comma* (Comma, 2003), edited by Ra Page. 'Beginning' was first published in *Decapolis*, edited by Maria Crossan (Comma Press, 2007). 'Getting Home (The Proofreader's Sigh)' was first published in *Closure* (Peepal Tree Press, 2015), edited by Jacob Ross. 'Rats and Mice' was first published in *Rainy City Stories* (2008), edited by Kate Feld and Chris Horkan. A version of 'Contents May Vary' was first published in *Lotus-eater* magazine (2022). A version of 'Soul Sisters' was first published in *Mrs Pinto Drives to Happiness* (Dahlia Publishing, 2021).

First published in Great Britain in 2024 by Comma Press.
www.commapress.co.uk

A CIP catalogue record of this book is available from the British Library.

ISBN-10: 1905583117
ISBN-13: 9781905583119

The publisher gratefully acknowledges the support of Arts Council England.

Supported using public funding by

ARTS COUNCIL
ENGLAND

In partnership with Manchester UNESCO City of Literature

City of Literature

Printed and bound in England by Clays Ltd, Elcograf S.p.A

MIX
Paper | Supporting responsible forestry
FSC® C013604

Contents

CONTENTS

Introduction

WE MANCUNIANS HAVE A rather curious approach to identity. On one hand, we can be intensely specific about a person's Mancunian status: is someone from Manchester or Salford? (Two separate cities, never forget.) Do folks from Tameside, Oldham and Bury even qualify as 'proper Mancs'? Then there are those all-important cultural markers – like, does one say 'chip barm' or 'chip butty'? (the latter, *obviously*).

Conversely, Mancunians can also take a far more fluid, inclusive approach to civic pride. Just consider how supporters of those two footballing behemoths, United and City, have embraced the likes of Ole Gunnar Solksjær, Eric Cantona or Vincent Kompany, passionately regarding those 'foreign imports' as one of our own. And it's not just elite footballers we take to our hearts, but all those who arrive in the city to make their mark, their contribution, who choose to call this place their home. From the days of the Industrial Revolution, which kickstarted large-scale immigration to the city, to the thousands of students who arrive here each September, the city has long possessed an international aura. And, from my own experience, native Mancunians have always been quick to recognise and celebrate what all those 'adopted' and 'honorary' Mancs bring to the city.

It's this spirit of inclusion that firmly underpins *The Book of Manchester.* A collection consisting of people who were born and bred here, joined by writers who came from elsewhere in the UK, or other countries, and made Manchester their home. Homegrown Mancs and honorary Mancs working and playing side-by-side – very much a microcosm of the city as we know it.

The common denominator between all those writers is a deep, profound affection for the city, albeit one tempered with an acute understanding of its myriad flaws and contradictions. Indeed, one might say that's the ultimate quality that defines all Mancunians, homegrown or adopted – an ability to be bursting with civic pride whilst having a good old moan about the city, often within the same sentence. The twelve stories contained within, we hope, will attest to that nuanced, complex relationship.

The story of Manchester's literary history is, of course, populated with great writers – both native and non-native - who strived to get beneath its surface, to show the city for what it truly is, unfettered and unvarnished.

The city that gave the world its first glimpse of the Industrial Revolution also, crucially, provided a literary window through which to examine those times of social and political upheaval. *Mary Barton*, the first novel by Elizabeth Gaskell (1810-1865) showed the extreme poverty and hardship that arose as a result of the rapid industrialisation during the mid-nineteenth century. Gaskell's close acquaintance, Charles Dickens, is believed to have written his 1854 novel *Hard Times* after observing the appalling working conditions in the factories and mills of Manchester and Preston. Isabella Banks (1821-1897) is most widely remembered for her novel *The Manchester Man*, which contained vivid accounts of the Peterloo Massacre and Corn-law riots. And, most famously, the German-born philosopher Friedrich Engels (1820-1895) penned his highly influential work *The Condition of the Working Class in England* when he lived in the city for several decades,

carefully honing his radical philosophies as he studied the slums of Victorian-era Manchester.

Beyond social writing, the city has also proven to be a versatile backdrop for genre practitioners. For Harpurhey-born Anthony Burgess (1917-1993), the city's Moss Side gangs of the 1920s and 1930s apparently inspired his iconic 'droogs' in *A Clockwork Orange* (1962). For Tameside author Jeff Noon, Manchester's early-nineties nightlife scene played backdrop for his dystopian, drug-addled debut *Vurt* (1993). And, more recently, in Joseph Knox's 2017 debut *Sirens* (2017) the crime-ridden city centre plays host to an unsettling, compelling work of 'Manc noir'.

In recent decades, Manchester's literary allure has been firmly intertwined with its academic institutions: the University of Manchester's Centre for New Writing and MMU's Manchester Writing School effectively serving as a conveyor belt for top-class writing talent and future literary prize winners.

Allied to its impressive array of iconic, literary locations (Central Library, the Portico, John Rylands, Working Class Movement Library), an ever-growing line-up of independent publishers (Carcanet, Commonword, Saraband, Northodox and Fly On The Wall), and a healthy live literature scene, it's hardly surprising that Manchester was named the 26th UNESCO City of Literature in 2017, joining the likes of Milan, Melbourne and Barcelona.

Objectively speaking, Manchester's literary heritage – and, by extension, its ever-thriving creative industries – has undoubtedly enhanced the city's international status. However, at what point does one decide that a particular aspect of a city's development is a good thing, a sign of positive progression, and when it's not; when is it something that may be detrimental to a city and its residents?

As someone who has lived and worked in the city for most of my forty-plus years, I've witnessed much of Manchester's recent transformation(s) up close. The most significant of those changes undoubtedly came in the aftermath of the IRA bomb that ripped through the city's central shopping area on Saturday 15th June, 1996. That event is seen by many as the catalyst for Manchester's modern rebirth, the city undergoing its most ambitious urban facelift since 1945. At the time, I can recall people speaking feverishly about a 'Mancunian renaissance': the ubiquitous redbrick and broken windows of the previous decades making way for fancy loft apartments, the new Printworks complex, and a glitzy red carpet heralding the then-upcoming Commonwealth Games.

But fast forward to 2024 and the city's powers of recovery, its innate ability to harness culture and leisure to make itself relevant and attractive – and, most importantly, profitable – has proven altogether more divisive. A decade on from then-Chancellor George Osborne's plans for a 'northern powerhouse', Manchester city centre has undergone seismic redevelopment, thanks in large part to a billion-pound property boom. In 1990, the city centre population was only around 500; in 2024, it's close to 60,000 – a truly staggering transformation. Where once Manchester only boasted one notable skyscraper, the 25-storey CIS Tower built in the 1960s, these days one can see tower blocks and skyscrapers in every direction. These opulent edifices might be seen by some as signs of a thriving urban metropolis, a successful modern economy, evidence that Manchester's smart pragmaticism has, once again, paid rich dividends. Others, however, will point to the sheer vulgarity of what is often referred to as 'Manctopia', claiming that the city centre has become little more than a playground for property developers, and that affordable housing is simply not an option for ordinary Mancunians. Gentrification, as with so many major UK cities, has only widened the gulf between the haves and have-nots. At a time when the international spotlight is being focussed on Manchester like never before – those extravagant Chanel fashion shows in the Northern Quarter, the opening of the Co-op Live arena, the city's famous nightlife and footballing dominance – the Mancunian mood is considerably more cynical than chest-beating.

It would be an over-simplification to say that all twelve stories gathered here interrogate this ambivalence – that constant push-and-pull between being immensely proud of the city's ever-growing reputation, and being suspicious of 'progress'. But what these stories do achieve is a narrative intimacy within the much larger picture of a city undergoing significant change. And, in true Mancunian fashion, they pull no punches when it comes to deep, serious examination of the city's recent growth.

Nowhere is this approach better encapsulated than in Sophie Parkes' 'Shock City', an unsettling tale in which present-day, latte-sipping Ancoats collides with a chilling echo of Victorian-era Manchester. The city's growing property empire is also alluded to in Okechukwu Nzelu's 'The Headteacher', a sharply observed comedy of manners about the husband of a retiring headmaster entertaining colleagues and former pupils at his new home in Altrincham. Reshma Ruia's 'Soul Sisters', meanwhile, looks at how one's own personal insecurities can be amplified in the face of a rapidly changing city. Elsewhere, the idea of Manchester as seen from an outsider's perspective is explored in Bronte Schiltz's 'Contents May Vary', which shows how the city can gradually, gracefully become a sanctuary for non-Mancs who relocate here. By contrast, Peter Kalu's 'Getting Home (The Proofreader's Sigh)' describes the experience of a born-and-bred Mancunian, who, because of the colour of his skin, doesn't feel entirely safe walking his own streets at night.

Outside of contemporary settings, *The Book of Manchester* also contains a clutch of stories exploring both Manchester's recent past and speculative futures. Tom Benn's 'The Cat's

Mother' is an origin story-of-sorts for his acclaimed Henry Bane series, set in 1980s crime-laden Wythenshawe, and it's every bit as visceral as we've come to expect from the Stockport native's previous works. Mike Duff, one of Manchester's most overlooked writers, reflects on a lost childhood memory with the vituperative 'Rats and Mice' – not so much a short story as a punch to the solar plexus. Looking ominously to the future, Ian Carrington's 'Ten-Two Forty-Two' imagines a Manchester excised of all sense of community – a post-digital hellscape in which two once-close siblings can barely recognise each other.

Two stories explore themes of absence in relation to Manchester. The great Shelagh Delaney's 'Abduction', about a teenage boy unwittingly wrenched from his family and hometown, leaves the reader to wonder what regional dislocation and lure of London does to families generally. While Yusra Warsama's 'Cloaks' maps out what's lost exactly when the dead hand of gentrification reaches into once proudly multicultural, working-class areas like Moss Side.

The idea of Manchester as a city of curious dichotomy – a place of simultaneous great expanse and sometimes unnerving proximity – is explored in the two stories that bookend this collection. David Constantine's 'Beginning', which opens the book, finds an older, rueful narrator reflecting on his daily journeys home from school during postwar Manchester. Whilst rich in geographical detail (the River Irwell has surely never been described so hauntingly), it's ultimately a story of close encounters, of those intense, fateful experiences that can forever define one's relationship to a city. Likewise, Mish Green's 'Occupy Manctopia', which closes the collection, is an all-too believable examination of those below-the-breadline citizens invariably left behind by any big city's predilection for all-things new and shiny. Yet, as its title suggests, 'Occupy Manctopia' is a story not without hope or defiance, one that taps into Manchester's proud traditions of protest and social justice. There may, after all, be buoyant community amidst the rampant commodity.

Finally, on a personal note, I must admit to feeling an overwhelming sense of responsibility – and fear! – when I was initially tasked with editing *The Book of Manchester*. Comma Press' Reading The City series has so far published over 25 editions, and those collections have all been thrillingly consistent in delivering top-tier stories about their respective destinations. Despite Manchester being the home and birthplace of Comma, this book has been a long time coming. Well, the wait is finally over, and whether by luck or design, this book has arrived at a time when the city is at a hugely significant crossroads. I hope that these twelve stories in some way reflect that critical juncture – and, most importantly, do justice to the city I am proud to call home.

David Sue
Manchester, September 2024

Beginning

David Constantine

Coming home from visiting my mother, distressed that she no longer knows who I am and cannot make any sounds that I recognise as words, I set down the odd fact that on this day 45 years ago, 31 May 1961, coming home from school under blue skies, I saw my first dead fellow human being. He was in the river under Victoria Bridge where I caught my second bus, the 64 or the 66. I was seventeen. I've seen few dead since then, far fewer than the averagely unlucky seven-year-old in Gaza or Baghdad has already seen. I had a good look at him. Scores of people were leaning over the parapet and doing the same. I looked and looked. And when I got home I wrote him up in my notebook, that drowned man.

On the first bus, the 42 from Birchfields Road to Albert Square, I sometimes met a girl and we sat together, if we could. Our meetings weren't arranged but they weren't entirely accidental either. I worked out which buses were most likely on which days, and went for those. But once on a bus I had no hope about, nearly an hour later than our usual times, there she was. So really I never knew. We sat upstairs, if there was room, with the smokers. Often it was sunny and the curls, the ringlets, the spiralling, floating, unravelling tresses of bluish smoke in the beams of sun made a pretty effect. I say often, but

1

I don't suppose I saw her more than a dozen times. I never even knew her name. All I know is it began with 'M'. She'd be there already, if it was a lucky day, sitting upstairs in the sunny smoke and saving me a place next to her on the front seat, if we were especially lucky. All we talked about was books, and I never touched her except in the way you are bound to if you sit next to somebody on a bus and you turn and forget yourself in conversation. I remember her eyes, the soul staring out of them, eager and scared, and I remember her lips and tongue but not any single sentence that she said, only the tone, the rhythms, the feel of her speech, so close, the aura of her. She got off a couple of stops before me, near Central Station, and of course I don't know where she went from there. A couple of days before I saw the man in the river she gave me a present, as she was getting off. She took it out of her satchel as she stood up, thrust it at my heart, and was gone. I never saw her again.

I didn't open the girl's present until I was upstairs on the 64 on Victoria Bridge. The buses started from there and you might have to wait a while before they were due to leave. All the years I was going to school, and for many before that, so I am told, there was a madman on Victoria Bridge, called Charlie. He wore the cap and jacket of a sort of uniform and he believed himself to be in charge of the comings and goings of the buses on Victoria Bridge. He had a pocket watch, that he consulted frequently, and a notebook, and one of those pencils you have to keep licking to get it to write. The soldiers had them in the First World War. So Charlie, who might have been in his sixties at that time, stood all day and every day, rain or shine, on Victoria Bridge, waving the big green buses in and out, consulting his watch, shaking his head, and very frequently licking his bit of pencil. Everyone was nice to him. All the drivers and conductors acted along, pretending he was in charge, and even the real supervisor, who had a little office on the bridge, took it in good part and you might see the pair of them, the real one and the mad one, in a slack time sharing tea from a thermos. But that day I didn't look at Charlie, though I normally did, looked and looked, I sat on the front seat, from where you had a view, if you wanted it, of Telephone House on your right, Exchange Station and the cathedral on your left, the dirty river under you, and I undid the girl's present which she had wrapped very carefully and tied up with a red ribbon. I believe I was alone on the upper deck. I believe all behind me was empty space.

It was a Wilfred Owen she had given me, and on a scrap of paper, that looked torn out of a Woolworth's notebook, she had written: Here are his poems for you. With love from M. That was when I learned her name began with 'M'. First I looked to see how long the poet had lived. I had taken to doing that. I saw that if I were him I'd be two-thirds through my allotted time already. Then I opened his book, nowhere particular, as I thought, and the space behind my back filled up with cold, it felt like a finger tracing my spine and inserting a tip of cold into the back of my head so that the hairs stood up there, I had ice around the heart and I lost the sight of his lines in a rush of tears. Then Charlie consulted his pocket watch, waved us away, licked his blue copy-pencil and made a note in his notebook of the exact time of day that particular 64 left Victoria Bridge for Peel Green.

The Irwell is the boundary between Manchester and Salford. The buses leaving Victoria Bridge cross it, back into Manchester, bear left along it past the cathedral and the station, and, turning sharp left, cross it again, back into Salford, and away. The man had been in the water for some time when I joined the others watching, and a couple of frogmen were in there with him, trying to push his head and shoulders through a lifebelt, to haul him up. They had a hard task, he was so sodden and unhelpful. One took his head by the hair and tugged. The face was blue-grey. I realised that must be one of the colours of death, nothing that colour could be alive, or not in any way friendly to human beings at least. Though I didn't know I would never see M. again – it was only a couple of days since she had given me the poems and we often went that long or longer without meeting – I was already beginning to be anxious. I had to talk to her about Wilfred Owen; and while I was watching the men in the water under Victoria Bridge I was wondering whether I should tell her about this event, and how I would say it if I decided to.

High above the river, just below street level, on a rather ramshackle platform affixed to the bridge, two policemen were watching their colleagues in the water and handling the ropes by which the drowned man was to be hauled up. I thought you might get to the platform through the supervisor's little office on the street side of the parapet. Had the river been a sweeter place he and Charlie might have taken their tea out there, on a balcony with a view. Friedrich Engels, working just round the corner in Chetham's Library on *The Condition of the Working Class in England*, thought the river and its dwelling-places supremely noxious. Poor river, it had a coal mine at the very outset and more and more demands and abuses through the cotton towns below. All its tributaries harmed it. But there were blessings nonetheless, reprieves and survivals, woods, for example, beyond the sewage farm at Clifton, and bluebells in season, hyacinthine streams and pools, like a surrogate living water. For the body of the Irwell was largely effluent, it needed what humans spilled into it to keep going at all. The rain itself came heavily laden and before it reached the river must take on the further cargo of the gutters and the drains. The Irwell was never much of a waterway, and under the bridge and the sheer side of Telephone House there was little movement. Of his own accord, so to speak, the drowned man might have idled for ever in the dead stillness under Victoria Bridge.

The policemen took off their jackets and began to haul. In shirt-sleeves on that dismal perch they looked like snowbirds. The drowned man, fitted through the lifebelt, rose in the water into a semblance of buoyancy, but very soon after that, when he was tiptoe on the surface as though they were puppeteers and now they would get him to dance, the operation went wrong. The deadweight of him was too much for their arrangement of ropes. He slipped from the ring and was upended, noosed tightly around the ankles, the ring banging uselessly against his back. Water returned to the river from his jacket sleeves. We could smell it. There he hung, his clothes undoing around his midriff, hung and twirled very slowly, streaming. The frogmen assessed him. The police on the platform waited. It seemed his ropes would hold. It seemed they must risk it. At a signal, again they began to haul. Abattoir, martyrdom, circus, theatre, ascension. We were all very quiet. I decided I would tell the girl on the bus what I was seeing. I thought of the words. I felt certain she would understand what was happening to me while I watched. Suddenly there was a rush of things I must tell and ask the girl on the bus. Was her grandfather a soldier? Was his name in the book in the cathedral? And all the things my mother had begun to tell me, about the Blitz, how she and her best friends in Telephone House had volunteered to carry on working during a raid and the searchlights lit up the sky and soon they could hear the guns and the bombs. And her and my father courting: Ringley Woods, the bluebells, and how in the leap year 1936, egged on by the other girls, while the supervisor's back was turned, she phoned him at his work in the Post Office from hers on the top floor of Telephone House, and asked him to marry her. Things of that sort, so much, so many stories, all in a rush. By way of thanks for the poems of Wilfred Owen. Tell her and ask her. The drowned man twirled very slowly upside down in the lovely light of day, the water still running off him, a precious silver. And slowly he rose, with pauses, with rests in the air, hanging down, his hands come together like a diver's, everyone watching, all silent.

It was perhaps the beginnings of my father's illness that

made my mother, that spring and summer, begin to tell me stories about the two of them in their early lives. He was slipping into something that neither of them understood and perhaps she wanted to assure herself of him by saying aloud how definite and luminous still their beginnings were. The remoteness of depression is hard to bear. Some acts of suicide in it may spring from the desire to be finally definite again. All the more definite around the depressive must the people who love him be, and perhaps that was an unconscious motive in my mother's stories: to make me her ally in knowing some things for sure. The cheerfulness of the girls high up in Telephone House was one such thing, how she proposed to him in the leap year with some of them watching her face for the answer in it and some further off watching out for the supervisor. And under the air raid all together, the lights and the noise, that was a brave thing to remember when it looked as though isolation by an illness might be coming up. But I liked best her assertion that on a clear day from the top floor of Telephone House she could see Ringley Woods where they went picking bluebells and came back on the bus with an armful and she slept against his shoulder in the scent of them lying in her lap like a child. And beyond Ringley, on a clear day, you could see the moors, level and high, and once up there, as is well known, you can walk out together for ever.

That spring and early summer, now I come to think of it, there must have been something about me that was asking for stories, because if it wasn't my mother telling them it was her mother and I stood or sat or strolled between the generations of women and listened to whatever they wanted to tell me about the girls at Ermen and Engels Mill or Telephone House and courtships before the first war or the second, long courtships, engagements, marriages. I watched my father anxiously, willing him with my mother not to go absent on us, and my grandfather – 'blown to bits', as his widow said whenever she reached that point, said with a shrug – him, my mother's father, I was beginning to put together again, his life till then, till the blowing to bits, collecting him up, so to speak, from her bits of story and the documents. So to speak. There is no liveliness of words comes anywhere near the life of life itself.

At the last, the drowned man's feet caught under the platform and one policeman had to kneel, leaving the other taking all the weight. It was only then I noticed that he wore decent Oxford shoes. He turned my way, his tie hung over his open mouth. They meant no indecency, I am sure, but in getting their burden over the railing of the rickety platform they could not be gentle. They reached, heaved, landed him. He lay then over the railings, arms down and between his arms his head, the hair neatly plastered forward by the foul water in a V. He wore a suit. He was perhaps in his mid-forties. I could see him with a briefcase, conscientiously going to work and back. The policeman left him there, flopped, as though after a tremendous exertion mortally exhausted. They exited through the supervisor's office and soon returned with a stretcher. Then it was finished, the spectacle. The crowd remembered their own business.

I went for my bus, a 66, got the front right seat upstairs, and craned up to see the very roof of Telephone House. There was a white cloud or two, the high building seemed to be sailing. The bus filled up, mostly young women from their work, nattering and laughing. On the bridge the ambulance had taken the drowned man away; the policemen, still in their dazzling shirtsleeves, were having a cup of tea. Things were resuming, but not fast enough for Charlie. I doubt if he had watched the spectacle at all. He was in the road itself before the queue of buses, very agitated, tapping his watch and shaking his head. Suicide's one thing, but what about the buses? What about the timetable? His trouble was manifest and helpless. My pity, quickened by one thing and another, went out to him there on the public bridge in such an anxiety. He beckoned hard, stepped aside, we pulled away. I watched him lick his pencil and make the necessary note. Mustn't forget Charlie when I tell all this to the girl on the 42.

Getting Home

A Black Urban Myth
(The Proofreader's Sigh)

Peter Kalu

STRANGE THINGS HAPPEN AFTER midnight. Three weeks ago, a Friday, I was coming back from London. Earlier trains had been cancelled and I was in this crowded last train. We were all crammed in, my mouth was dry as feathers, my stomach twisted with hunger. I got out at Manchester Piccadilly, uncreased myself, and headed to the city centre bus stop on Oldham Rd[1] to get back to Oldham where I live.

OK, nobody rushes to get back to Oldham. There are no flowing cornfields, no marble terrazza[2] leading to sublime waterfalls in which bronze demigods frolic, no sumptuous hot sand beaches up which fishermen haul their boats, land and fry their catch to the praise songs of waiting villagers. Nevertheless, it is home; there is a lockable door there for me and, behind that, a decent mattress.

I must have dozed on the train like a horse[3], sleeping on my feet. The train must have been further delayed en route because it

---

1. Sic. Fact check: actually Oldham Street.
2. Sic. Cannot mean *terrazza* as in balcony. Probably means *passaggio* (walkway) though these are never marble.
3. Sic. Generally, horses are not found dozing on trains.

9

was later than I'd thought – the battery on my phone had no-barred me somewhere between Stoke-on-Trent and Crewe[4] so I couldn't check the time.

Waves of cleaners were slipping in and out of office blocks. McDonalds[5] had placed a security guard on their door. I get knocked into 'no offence, like' by some burly bloke. A girl – a buttery mix of cigarette, alcohol and Chanel No. 5 – ran up and kissed me, no doubt for a dare and I didn't fight it. Someone was dry-heaving by the Spar All Night Kiosk.[6] It was that kind of late. The air was some strange miasma[7] – a balmy cocktail of pepperoni pizza fumes and the convecting heat of a long, hot day was infusing the night with good vibes. Mancunians are not used to this – heat – and they're all a bit thrown. I drag my weary ass through it all, clutching my flight bag of poetry publisher's proofs. As I walk, I reel off a couple of Inshallaahs, God Willings[8] and pluck the entrails of a sacrificial chicken in my sleep-addled mind, before stepping up to the podium, face oiled, every one of my twisted dreads in immaculate place as I ask, please, no more applause, I am not worthy, my poems are not worthy…[9]

It was only when I got to the bus stop I realised that the regular buses had stopped. I looked around. There were six of us huddled there, or spread about, waiting; only one of us, me, was sober. There is no greater hell than being the only sober person at a bus stop after Friday night's pub and club chuck-out time. Everyone's heaving or bawling or boasting. Nobody but you can read the bus timetable. I could feel a long line of zeds waiting to rush my brain; I could

---

4. Sic. No London trains call at both Stoke-on-Trent and Crewe. Probably means Stafford and Crewe.

5. Sic. Fact check: there is no McDonalds between Manchester Piccadilly and Oldham Street.Sic.

6. See Note 5. No Spar All Night Kiosk either.

7. Sic. Miasma is an unpleasant smell. Prob. means ether.

8. Repetition: Inshallah means God willing.

9. I am not paid enough to untangle the confusion of tenses in this paragraph.

feel my consciousness slipping off like petals from a fading flower; I could feel the God of Sleep arriving in her spray-gold Chariot.[10] A not unpleasant numbness was just beginning to settle over me when the bus shelter frame shook and the glass I was leaning on shuddered.

This tattooed knucklehead, at least 40, staggers up to me – big chops, red face, rubber legs. He has this wary, I'm-a-hard-man-just-finished-my-prison-sentence-for-GBH look. He sways past me and he's in front of the timetable board at the bus stop, squinting.

He turns to me. 'When's the next bus?'

It's a bark, a command. Maybe he's ex-military, I muse; there were many around now – damaged in mind and body – after all the illegal British wars.

'According to the timetable it's at half past twelve – half past midnight,' I say, smiling at him.

'What time is it now?' he snaps back, swaying – which is a hard trick to pull off.

'Yeah, when's it comin'?' someone else calls out.

I'm wearing jeans and a black jacket. I don't have a clip board or walkie-talkie or anything, but everyone seems to think I work for the bus company. Maybe it's my rahtid[11] flight bag.[12] My mouth opens to tell them all to go fuck themselves, then closes again. I shrug off my zeds. The Windrushers[13] arrived in Britain and became bus conductors. Although my roots are African – not West Indian – this subtlety is for another time. I bow to my role. This is honouring our predecessors. We are born to conduct buses.

'It's half past,' I say, 'bus should be along any minute.'

There's a row of three young women, not past twenty, on the

---

10. Sic. Perhaps a reference to the Greek God Hypnos (male). No reference in antiquity to him ever arriving in a gold chariot, whether sprayed, dipped or painted.
11. Jamaican patois. Yet later narrator says he is of African heritage?
12. If he slept like a horse, perhaps saddlebag is better here than a flight bag? He has after all stepped off a train, not a plane.

doorway steps behind the bus stop. Standing by them are two lads[14] – the boyfriends I presume – both swaggering drunk, giving mouth[15] to whoever passes by. One of them, the slightly heavier one, has a long stick by his side, like a cue stick. A Pakistani-looking bloke my age, still in kitchen whites under his coat, comes along. He pauses at the stop, takes in the scene and, wisely perhaps, carries on walking. So I'm still the only sober guy here.

And I'm the only one who's not white, not that anybody's mentioned this so far. I've been around the world; I can handle the situation.

The two boyfriends get a quarrel going with a couple of bouncers standing outside the King's Head just four doorways down. I thought bouncers were trained to be calm and negotiate a situation without violence. These must have been on holiday when they ran that course. The boyfriend with the cue stick that isn't a cue stick starts doing these Bruce Lee kung fu moves, goading the bouncers. His mate is bopping about like the old style boxers used to. The bouncers are huge. The two lads are puny. Do I intervene? Are you crazy? I decide I can do without the bus, it's only ten miles.[16]

As I walk on there are various yelps, expletives, splinterings and ejaculations coming from the vicinity of the nightclub doors. I'm about to turn round but… nah, still not worth it. If people's sense of fun extends to rushing at bouncers to get their heads busted, so be it.

I look down the road to Oldham. It's a vast, bleak, empty landscape, known locally as Miles Platting. And now rain.

I suppose in this situation, for some, a hotel becomes a viable

---

13. Only reference I can find to Windrushers is to a UK gliding club. Were they blown off course? I suggest cut or rephrase.

14. Maths is not this writer's strong suit, I suspect. So far seven people 'at or around' bus stop including himself, not six, as stated earlier.

15. Is this a Northern expression? It reads as slightly sexual, or is that just me? Suggest rephrase or omit.

16. The tenses are all over the place in this paragraph. Again.

option. In my eyes, I am a promising young black poet with several publications under his belt, on the cusp of literary and financial greatness. In the mean eyes of the grasping telephone loan arrangers, I am no more than a 37-year-old Lancastrian with fifteen years of sporadic missed payments who, *if I may speak off the record, sir, would be best advised to change career. The poetry obviously does not pay; after fifteen years, even you can do the maths on that one, with respect, sir.*

Yeah, right. Expensive loans but free careers advice.[17]

So, I'm walking home out of the city centre along Oldham Rd. It's 2am-ish, dark, light rain – par for the course for Manchester. The street is deserted. I walk on and on. The rain keeps it up. A white woman comes into view on the same side of the street.

The navigation of public space by a lone black male in the night is problematic with or without hoodies, with or without 'stand-your-ground' laws, with or without a Neighbourhood Watch committee in place – or whether or not that space is 'gated', should we say? Likewise, the ability (as opposed to the right) of a lone woman to move unmolested through the night in whatever kit she's decided to don. I nudge my zeds[18] aside and try to process the information provided by my eyes. From this distance, she could be a very light-skinned black woman, in which case she might give me a short nod of recognition as we glide past each other, our black solidarity thing boosted. She is in a party dress. (I would like to provide more information on the dress: e.g. an A-line bolero effect with diamante detail and a flounced flapper hemline, scrunched at the midriff, clutched at the waist, and single shoulder strap. But a man's got to know his limitations. It was a dress. A party dress.)[19]

You can speculate why she is walking late at night:

A party just finished and no taxi money?

---

17. Good advice for this writer. Every so often someone at a call centre speaks sense.

18. Infelicitous?

19. Should either describe the dress or not. Brackets become annoying. Dress as described is a logical impossibility.

A lover's tiff?

She's her auntie's main carer and needs to get back to help her auntie dress in the morning?

Kids to get to school?

The gap between us is closing and I can see now she is alabaster white. Her body language – a stiffening of the back, a slight drop in the head, a faltering in her footwork – tells me we two are not about to duet to the soundtrack of *Fame*. Her increasing hesitation makes me decide that out of consideration for her, conscious of her vulnerability, and to make it easy for us both, I'll cross to the other side of the street. But she must have had the same idea. Just as I cross, she crosses too. She's convinced now I'm after her. We're on the same side of the street again and closing. She crosses the road again and starts walking back in the direction she has just come – slowly at first, then faster till she's running. Running away from me along the deserted London Rd.[20] Ah well, I did my best.

It's 2 something a.m.. The light rain has lightened into almost a mist.

Beauty is everywhere, even on the road to Oldham. I come across a scene that slides my eyebrows up my forehead and bunches my cheeks. Rabbits. Like a scene out of *Watership Down*, a hundred rabbits are bobbing up and down, nibbling grass on the wide roadside verge where the Italian Restaurant used to be before they flattened it for lack of custom. By day, this arterial road roars with lorries, commuters, bankers, fish vans, prison vans, car-parts couriers, mobile hairdressers. And lo, by night, there appear jug-eared, white, bob-tailed, jerky-up-and-down, fluffy, cuddly-toyable, cookable rabbits. I've stopped. They look at me. I look at them. They dart, then sit. Dart, then sit. Like my career, or Jockey Wilson[21] (Prince of the Flighted Arrow).

---

20. Sic. It was Oldham Rd a couple of paragraphs earlier. Fact check: no London Rd in Manchester leads to or from Oldham.

21. Darts player. Died 2012. Fact check: his nickname was 'Jocky'. Can find no reference to him being 'the prince of the flighted arrow'.

Misty rain is the long distance walker's dream. This is the mist rain of my high school's feeble showers, the mist rain of a dog's sneeze, the mist rain of a girlfriend's errant hair spray. It soothes the soul and coats my glasses so I have to keep taking them off and wiping them. It's while doing this that I turn the corner and there's a man, a white man, lying on the edge of the pavement. He's shouting, 'Help me! Help me!'

He looks in a bad way. Maybe a car has swiped him. It's wet, late. I'm tired, but you can't walk by. Did not that great Roman thinker, Thucydides[22] say it is the duty of every citizen to come to the aid of his brother? This is the very essence of our civilisation, the foundation stone of citizenship itself, without which the Barbarians will soon be clambering over our city walls, our temples to destroy, and we will all be hastened to hell in a handcart? Something like that.

He's seen me coming, and he's been trying, uselessly, to get up. All he needs is a helping hand. I shuffle my flight bag from one shoulder to the other, sweep my dreads off my face, bend down and offer my hand. He sees me close up and a mask of horror has installed itself on his face.

'Somebody else help me! Somebody else help me!' he shouts.

I pull back my hand and straighten up. Some civilisations deserve Barbarians inside their city walls.

This walking home business is not so simple, I decide. Maybe I should try hailing a cab. Three empty taxis have gone past in the last half hour of my walking, all of them heading back to the city centre. Surely they would want to make a little more money before calling it quits for the night? But I've got no cash. There's a Post Office close by with a cash machine in its wall. No one around. No one to panic. I put my card in the machine. A police car screams round the corner.

'Stay right there! Hands where I can see them!'

It's three something a.m., light rain, dark. I'm tired. 'OK.'

_____

22. Sic. Thucydides was Greek; need I say more? The entire reference is a load of cobblers, containing as many errors as you can shake a stick at.

I'm too wet to run anyway.

While they're questioning me – who I am, where I live – a car with no headlights comes screaming round the corner and smacks into a bus stop, concertinas it, then catapults into a lamp post that crashes into the road.[23]

'You going to see to that?' I ask the cops. 'You could do me later?'

They hate advice.

'We're doing fine here,' they say. 'Now, how long have you lived at this address and what is your mother's maiden name?'

They continue frisking me. There's blood oozing from the wrecked car, groans, but they display a complete insouciance to that. Once they've crawled all over me so they can recognise me in the dark by the shape of my frozen genitals, they let me go and proceed to the RTA23.

I turn to continue my transaction with the global capitalist system but my card has disappeared. Yeah. Still, the cops who frisked me found a tenner in my back pocket and handed it to me, though they kept my little bag of herbs.

I walk on, watching to hail a cab. For the same reason – known only to God – that buses do this – several come at once. The first has an 'I Heart Pakistan' sticker. It flies right past me – en route to Lahore I suppose. The second cab's driven by a huge Rasta. He appears to be pulling over, then speeds up and off. 'Heh, heh, heh!' Yes, Rasta, you can laugh. The third cab has this bald-headed, olive-skinned guy at the wheel. He veers towards me, only to speed through this mother of a puddle, drenching me. In the back of that third cab I distinctly see the woman who fled back on London Road and the guy who'd been knocked over. The woman is waving my plastic cash card at me. And the guy's waving my little bag of herbs. As I'm taking all this in, the late night bus, all its lights off, flies past me, empty.[24]

---

23. No local newspaper articles cover this accident and I can find no official crime report on it.
24. Finished? Thank God!

Abduction

Shelagh Delaney

I WANTED TO DO her in. Sitting on Piccadilly Station waiting to catch the London train, I thought seriously about it. I ran through every thriller I'd ever read and analysed the reasons why most of the murderers in them get caught. I reckoned that even if I did get caught it would be worth it. Capital punishment as a deterrent was long gone, so I wouldn't risk being executed. With time off for good behaviour, plus parole, I speculated that whatever sentence I got for what was obviously a justifiable crime would eventually be cut in half. That's how I was thinking. Seriously. Can you imagine anything more inane?

Putting murder aside in the case of Ann, I contemplated other means of humiliating her and exposing her for what she was - a killer.

She didn't kill with guns, knives, blunt instruments or poison. She used money and the power of her unwavering self-assurance that she was always right.

I'm all for building confidence and self-esteem into people but, with some characters, there's a moment when confidence turns into insolence, and self-esteem transmogrifies into dangerous self-importance. What made Ann cross that line doesn't matter. She did. That's what counts. I was her older sister by six years but I can't remember her being anything but a steamrolling know-all. I used to think it was because she was fat but after the birth of my first child I got fat too. It didn't noticeably turn me into a ruthless bully. But then, as my family increased I got thinner and thinner. She didn't.

She was proud of herself and her achievements. I'm not saying she wasn't entitled to be. She was a showpiece product of the state educational system that flourished in those 'good old days'. Like a lot of people, she believed more was expected of children when she was at school. Standards were higher. Teachers were better. Family life was superior, children enjoying a kind of security tragically lacking nowadays. Being only a few years older I remembered those days too but my recollections were a bit different.

Because she loved children she trained as a doctor, specialising in paediatrics. She was good at it. She lived for her work. She only regretted that most people don't have the sense to do what she'd done when she was a young woman and get themselves sterilised.

When the best job opportunity, working in a London children's hospital, came along, she couldn't get out of Manchester quick enough. Although she'd been born and brought up there it had never been good enough. There was only one place worth living. London. When she left the only things she took from home were photographs of me and the children, her brothers and a picture of our parents on their wedding day. Otherwise it was just the clothes she stood up. She was going to make a new start and intended kitting herself out in London.

'Don't worry about me spending money,' she told her anxious mother. 'What's it for?' We were all going to club together and buy her some housewarming gifts but when we saw her attitude, we decided not to bother and gave her our good wishes instead.

She bought a house in Kensington, where she still lives,

and soon settled down into the kind of life she had always wanted, a whirl of work, theatres, art galleries, and dinner parties. She even took up horse riding in Hyde Park at weekends.

When she felt she'd thoroughly established herself she went back to Manchester, kidnapped her sixteen-year-old brother, and brought him with her to live in London.

He'd been born late in our parents' marriage and was much younger than she was. Getting him to go away with her wasn't hard. He'd just left school. He had no qualifications. He didn't have a job. He didn't know what kind of a job he wanted. Like most teenagers, he hadn't much confidence in his mother and father and Ann, his sister, had all the answers. She also had a lovely house in London and plenty of money that she was extremely generous with. A pleasantly leafy but boring suburb of Manchester didn't stand a chance with this on offer, and more promised.

The speed and adroitness with which she had taken their son left his parents dazed in Manchester. It wasn't something they'd sat down as a family and discussed. As far as they were concerned, she'd come home for a weekend visit. Her Mother had cooked all her favourite meals, much enjoyed, and her father, a motor mechanic, had given her car a good going over and returned it to her with clean spark plugs.

When she stood on the front doorstep of the house she'd grown up in and announced that she was taking their youngest child to London they thought she meant for a holiday and were pleased. When she put them straight about that, assuring them she was taking him to live in London, hopefully forever, their jaws dropped. She laughed and told them they looked gormless standing there with their mouths open. Promising them she could give him a better future than they could, she smiled at their dumbstruck silence, told them not to worry, waved goodbye and drove away. Life in London was going to be great. No doubt about it.

Once his father got over the abruptness of his youngest child's leaving, he was on the phone, reminding the boy that there's no such thing as a free lunch. But the boy was sixteen years old and his sister was right. Life in London was great. No doubt about it.

Soon he was enrolled in college doing media studies. He had no interest in the media. He actually he despised it. But he knew his sister expected something of him and media studies seemed the lesser of all the evils that college offered. Ann was slightly disappointed. Her sights for him had been set on accountancy or the law.

But he 'wasn't the stuff' accountants and solicitors were made of. He liked sports and music. He loved dancing. He'd learnt gardening from his father and cooking from his mother. Because their parents were shy, his older brothers had taught him everything they knew. By the time he was sixteen he'd had plenty of experience in the field of sex, drugs, smoking and drinking.

It was a wonderful life. His sister gave him a generous allowance. When he overspent it she happily made up the shortfall. Her little brother, the family baby, needn't worry about money. She had plenty. She knew that money used wisely made sense. So long as everything was left in her hands everything would be all right. He laboured diligently at his media studies while ridiculing them in his heart.

Through her work as a paediatrician, Ann made friends with some very influential people. When her young brother left college they were delighted to help and found him a good job selling advertising space in *Nursing Times*. As a first job gift his sister bought him a black cashmere overcoat, six beautiful shirts, a made-to-measure suit and a briefcase. The first time he left his sister's house for the office he felt like a fool togged up in black cashmere and silk shirts. He didn't wear the coat again. He hung it in the back of his wardrobe and dumped the briefcase in a skip outside somebody's house with all the other rubbish they were clearing out, going back to the beat-up old Nike sports bag he'd brought from home and had used all through college.

Although he'd started working, his sister didn't cancel the allowance she gave him every month and wouldn't accept any money for his keep at home. He realised it was time to go solo and started looking for a place of his own. While he looked, he spent more and more time with his girlfriend, Marianne, who already had her own flat.

When Marianne got pregnant, his sister told them to get an abortion. After the abortion she, Ann, would find him a home of his own and, if necessary, pay for it.

When they came out of shock Marianne was amazed, furious and puzzled all at the same time. How could anyone behave with such brutal insolence?

'She's more like a possessive mother than a sister,' she told her him. 'Are you sure you're not really her baby? Did she have you while she was still a schoolgirl and's been passing herself off as your sister ever since?'

'I've often wondered about that,' he laughed. 'But my brothers and eldest sister remember Mum being pregnant.'

When the abortion didn't materialise and her brother and Marianne got married, Ann went from one extreme to the other, and became a dangerously doting aunt. When they told her to stop lavishing presents on their daughter she told them to butt out! She'd do as she liked. Reminded that she was, after all, only the girl's aunt, not her mother and father combined, Ann simply sneered. She knew what children needed and was more aware than they were of this particular child's needs.

When this particular child's mother threw her father out because of his alcoholism, it was almost a relief to him. He'd managed to conceal his addiction for years. Marianne was the first to break his cover. For eighteen months, she tried to help, but with no need for further concealment, he abandoned himself totally to the drink. He had to go.

His sister, admittedly disturbed by his heavy drinking, denied alcoholism. It was too strong a word to describe his problem. She was a doctor. Her little brother couldn't have turned into an alcoholic without her noticing. The very idea! Absurd.

She welcomed him back into her Kensington home. His job with the *Nursing Times* had gone a long time ago but there was nothing to worry about. Being unemployable need not cause him anxiety. She went on giving him the allowance she'd never stopped paying into his bank account, insisting on him living rent free, providing his food, doing his laundry and even buying his clothes. He didn't want her spending so much on him. 'It's only money,' she'd say. 'That's what it's for.' She reasoned that if he had no money at all he'd steal it. She couldn't have her brother thieving to buy his booze. She'd buy it for him.

In the middle of sorting out her brother's housing and financial needs, she took time to write a threatening letter to his wife. She was furious that Marianne had thrown her husband out of the family home. She told her sister-in-law she'd never considered her a fit mother. Should she, Ann, ever have cause to think that the child wasn't being brought up in a way that met with her approval, she would have no hesitation in reporting Marianne to the social services.

When Marianne gave this letter to her husband to read he was shocked for a moment. Then he laughed and said, 'Oh it's just Ann. You know what she's like. She's always over the top.'

It took Ann longer to accept her brother's alcoholism than it took him. So far as she knew there had never been an alcoholic in the family. She admitted briefly, but only to herself, that apart from her immediate family the rest of her relations were a mystery to her. She had aunts, uncles and cousins she'd never met and didn't want to meet.

Mum and Dad wanted to take him home and get him better there but the great bully-ball of their daughter's madness rolling over them flattened their resolve. She got him on the best rehab programme money could buy. It didn't work.

He was a tender man. To see him with his wife and daughter was to see a truly loving man. When he was sober. When *was* he sober? He kept a record of his dry days. He was sober most of 1999. He didn't even have a drink on Millennium night when his sister's party people, whose main aim was to get absolutely rat-arsed before the turn of the century had surrounded him. He'd wanted to run away then, run back home to his mother and father. Was it possible to start all over again, he'd kept asking himself. Could he keep the beautiful bits of his life, his daughter and his wife, and dispose of the rest? Start again? Be forgiven? The words sometimes vibrated in his head. Start again. Fresh start. A clean sheet. The first day of the rest of your life. A day at a time. I am an alcoholic. I am a recovering alcoholic. How many alcoholics can I be?

On Millennium Eve the people at his sister's party joined hands for 'Auld Lang Syne'. Although he wanted to avoid this ritual his sister dragged him into it. As the world left one century and entered another he was crying. His sister's hopes were high. He was getting better. Back to normal. She knew how long he'd been off the booze. She'd known it would turn out all right. It was her ambition to get his daughter back for him. Convinced that, with her contacts and her money, she could get control. Thus she dismissed Marianne, whom he loved, as nothing, a nobody.

He was dead six weeks later. She found him sitting in a rickety old striped deckchair at the bottom of the garden. He was dressed for the cold and the leafless tree he'd chosen to sit under creaked gently above him as the wind blew. In his old Nike sports bag on the frozen grass beside him, she found an opened bottle of whisky.

While he drank he'd thought about working with his father in the garden, cooking with his mother and sitting with her on the settee while they both watched *Coronation Street*. He'd remembered dancing with Marianne and how much he'd enjoyed it. He'd danced with his daughter too. They'd danced together all three of them round the flat in the kitchen, through the bathroom, the bedroom and the living room. Even in the street they'd danced. He'd smiled at the memory until his heart had stopped.

Shock City

Sophie Parkes

THE NOISE FROM THE bar began to rise. It always did at this time, a few drinks in, football results levelled. Sugary cider would usually be giving way, around now, to local lager that made itself known at the back of the throat. If he leant over the flat's glass-fronted balcony, he'd be able to confirm that the bloke in the dark pink t-shirt was Rufus. Claret or burgundy, Rufus would call it. Maroon.

He saw Rufus here in the Square most Saturdays. Since third year, or whenever it was he'd got to know Rufus, he had seen him here. He didn't even need to look over to confirm that one of the other points in Rufus' triangle would be Sam, but when he did, it was. Face to phone, personality like one. He'd had long enough, but he still hadn't decided whether he liked Sam, whether Sam liked him. Though it didn't matter either way, as they would continue to meet like this, in the Square, all of them, Rufus and a whole set of other familiar faces with their vaguely known backstories: employment status, far-flung hometown. Despite graduation slipping further into the past, they were all, people his age, oscillating around a preordained track. They had to be, else they wouldn't keep tripping over each other's trainers at every new night their mates were putting on, or each flat-warming they gathered at.

25

If he went down there, brought a pint out into the Square and sidled up to them, shielded his eyes from the sun, itself squinting between the concrete, steel and glass, he would not only be acknowledged but accepted, his opinions sought in too-loud voices and elongated vowels. Jules was probably there herself, one ear to a conversation she didn't care about, the other to the ground. She'd come in later, wanting to know how he was putting his twenties – 'his *youth*,' she'd said the other day, half-serious – to good use. 'We won't have this time again.' What was she planning for herself? And on what solid ground did she feel she could plan? Only last month he could've counted on a job to fill his days and his bank account – one major, robust thing that gave, if not credibility, something on which he could hinge other decisions: how to spend an evening, how to spend a weekend. Now the weekdays yawned into evenings, rolled over into weekends.

Jules would be envious. She was always in deficit of time; she worshipped freelancers, the people that had time on their side. 'But they're all from money, really,' she'd said, 'they'll all have parental financial advisers and inheritance, so it doesn't go tits up. The real working class can't afford to freelance.' But did the real working class rent these glassy pods above bars, with their mezzanines and Juliet balconies and bi-folds? He hadn't asked. Jules would find a new flatmate easy enough. She probably already had a list on her phone of potential back-ups.

The final fingers of sun receded. This was what the developers had envisaged: young men and women in clusters – he leant over the rail now, the cool of it seeping into the cotton of his shirt – talking, phones leaping in and out of pockets like fish in the restored streetlight, the white of t-shirts and trainers glowing. Viral laughter. Clean, sensible fingernails pulling at dyed hair or on chains gifted by lovers. Waterproof panniers at feet.

Rufus and Sam knew he lived up here, could simply turn their heads upwards to beckon him down to join them if they wanted. If one of them looked up and saw him watching, head lolled onto his arm now, the can warmed in his other hand, would they stop and point? Would that send a domino run of heads clicking upwards, fingers raised, eyes narrowed? Gawping. Is that the word they'd use about him? Something his nana would say. Voyeur. Peeping Tom. No, that wasn't right. He wasn't doing anything wrong. He wasn't doing anything.

Besides, they didn't look up. They didn't look anywhere, but at their phones, their feet, their beers, into the faces of the people they were speaking to. Why would they? The Square wasn't new, they came here all the time. Many of them even lived here. It was theirs, and only for a few short years if Jules was correct, before they all got up together and landed, collectively, elsewhere. The suburbs, perhaps. The countryside. Not him, he wouldn't be part of that transition. Not because he was contrary or independently minded, but because he couldn't really work out how he'd been carried here in the first place. He'd floated on the first wave that took him south of the city, then on another back up to the centre. Surely they could only take him so far. He couldn't spend a life being upped and set down, like breadcrusts on the canal. His parents couldn't make sense of it as it was.

Rufus had stepped backwards so he was in full view of the balcony. He raised a plastic glass to his lips, something dark, a porter or a stout, and didn't wince as he knocked it back. He paused to consider something the girl – woman – opposite him had posed, and rubbed at his beard. Sam interjected and the woman nodded, two large hoops swinging either side of her face. Rufus kept quiet. That's what he liked about him. Rufus had been expensively educated, he had mentioned rowing once, and seemed to know something about everything, but he didn't try to mire others in the fog of his wisdom like other people he'd met at university, or their friends who had subsequently come to join them after the lure of their own university cities had waned. People like Sam, who ensured their few, arbitrary opinions came with rehearsed, associated facts that made them sound like vehement truths. Jules could take him apart if she wanted.

But at least they *had* opinions. What did he know? He had been a novelty, when he was a kid, for his fervent support of Man City. Even that, now, had become dull. What could he say to a woman, a woman like Heidi that Sam was speaking to now, that would get her nodding, saying, 'Yes, *absolutely*?' Sam might be as flat as the phone he looked at, as binary as the computers he had studied, but he could at least offer Heidi something, judging by the way she was listening, joining in.

To Jules, he listened; she even teased him for it, for being so attentive. 'I'm brainwashing you, man. Do you listen to other women this closely?' She was right, of course. Everything he encountered for the first time – the invasion of Ukraine, Uber Eats, a craft beer – he'd assess it from her perspective first, before he felt he could take a line, which usually happened to be hers, anyway. Thankfully, he'd stopped blushing at her direct questions years ago. He was the pair of ears to whom she could outline burgeoning theories, appraise the shape and taste of her words before taking them out to more challenging environments, where she had to shout them over ribcage-bursting beats to the honed minds of postgraduate students.

Rufus, Sam and Heidi paused to drink and he mirrored them, upending the warm can into his mouth and wiping his lips with the back of his hand. Heidi looked at her watch. No doubt she had a shift at Jimmy's about to start. She left, Rufus and Sam shooting words between them as they watched her thread between the growing crowds. Which of them had fucked her? Perhaps both. Possibly neither. Their plastic glasses pushed into their midriffs, their blank faces told him nothing.

He opened a third can, no cooler than the others. He should've kept them in the fridge. He should take more care over things. He should value what he has. What he can afford to have. It's only Aldi beer. But this – this flat, this bar, this city – would've been unthinkable to his parents. Remained unthinkable. Manchester was a specific seasonal outing: Christmas shopping, a musical. Only soap stars lived there, university professors. His parents' visits had begun in regular earnest, but had slipped to every three months, longer. His mum had started speaking on his dad's behalf, Dad silently knifing his Elnecot pork belly.

'Your dad saw Tom's dad in Halford's the other day. Says he's doing really well at Telent, didn't he, love?'

'Your dad's been sorting through the garage. You won't believe what we've kept hold of over the years.'

'One of your old teachers got on your dad's bus the other week. Do you remember Mrs Stephens? She knew your dad right away, didn't she, love?'

Another group had found their way to Rufus and Sam now, as though they were guests of honour at a high society ball. They were used to it. *It is your turn to see Messrs. Rufus and Sam now.* Christ, he didn't even know their surnames. Rufus led this time and graciously gave way to the slender hands of a girl he had seen often enough, in the Square but also on her bike on Great Ancoats Street. He didn't know her name. Sam, demoted, took out his phone and thumbed his screen, stretched a leg out behind him, and rocked his weight forwards and back, forwards and back. Didn't he realise how ridiculous he looked? How rude? But the group didn't care. The conversation volleyed around him, Rufus again yielding to slender hands girl, other heads nodding or looking away before returning, scratching ankles, swatting flies. How did Sam get away with it? Did people – did his generation – simply expect listeners to duck in and out of conversations, resort to their phones when they could no longer be arsed?

Sam rocked again but with more vigour this time and knocked into a child. Yes, he looked closer, an actual child. A boy half Sam's size. Sam, still magnetised to his phone, didn't appear to notice but the boy did, wincing or shrugging or ducking at the contact, then continued his path through the knots of people.

He checked his phone. Nine fifteen. Did ten-year-olds stay up until gone nine? The families round here, it was a possibility.

He was so much shorter than Sam, though. Maybe he was younger than ten. Eight? Six? His hair was of no colour and long on top, stiff over his left eye and hacked about the ears. An older kid would be self-conscious of that. What eight-year-old would be out alone on a Saturday night? He scanned the clusters of people for a likely parent: a tall, out-of-place man, football belly under polo shirt, croaking about the price of beer. A woman, hair tight to her skull and vest straps cutting in to her skin. Jules would whistle at his snobbery. But he was only stating the obvious, the families round here; it wouldn't be unthinkable to find a belly straining against a polo shirt, or shoulders reddened by sunburn and bra straps. And besides, he *came* from a place of bellies and bra straps. He was allowed to say it; Jules, too. It'd be different if Rufus did.

The boy twisted into a gap recently vacated by four dark-haired sunglasses wearers, European tourists perhaps, or exchange students at the end of their stay. He had an attempt at a scarf at his neck, knotted fabric like a bandana, and his pants were too long for his twig legs, baggier at the bottom and held up by a vast brass buckle. As he broke into a run, his pants revealed bare feet slapping against the grey brick. It couldn't be. Not bare feet. He leapt up against the balcony for a closer look, but the boy was sucked into the lane beneath his block. Maybe it was a new fad, flesh-coloured shoes made to look like feet. *Fad.* Another Nana word. He waited for the parent or an older sibling maybe, to come elbowing through the crowds, bodies clashing, presence announced by coarse expletives. (Another stereotype, but a stereotype was a stereotype for a reason, right? And he'd witnessed it. He had lived experience.)

But the people in the Square didn't need to right themselves, didn't need to frown at the language or clutch the arms that had been roughed out of the way because nobody did come and the boy and his feet-shoes had escaped. Running because he was later than the curfew his parents had set. Running because he risked a grounding. Or running because

– and this had been his first thought, actually, but it was only now he was willing to test it, put it through the Jules-mill – he had stolen something, many things, from the flaccid back-pockets and gaping handbags of the people, the trusting boys and girls, the young, professional men and women, New Ancoats, that sprawled out across the Square.

Pickpocket. Nana word.

Sam put his phone away. Something in their talk had changed, had piqued his interest, and he leant forward, joined in. What would reel Sam in? The last conversation he'd been party to – it had been in the Square, of course it had, what, two, three Saturdays ago? When he was still at the agency and felt he could offer something to conversations – had been about the four-day week and the universal basic income. It was something that seemed to come up often, and he hadn't met anyone in the Square that wasn't in favour of it. Jules had been ecstatic. 'Imagine! People like my mum actually able to look after their grandkids and work and still maybe even have some time to themselves. It could be revolutionary!' Despite Rufus and Sam being from the kinds of families that chose when they worked and sent invoices afterwards for fees it would take Jules' mum months to accumulate, they were up for it, too. 'Starting everyone from the same base line,' Sam had said, to which Rufus had nodded enthusiastically. He had felt confused at that, as he often did when he knew there was an opposing thought burrowing away at his belly but he needed it to wriggle up, higher up, so he could give voice to it. By then, Jules had been at the bar, and when she returned, talk had moved to Starmer and he couldn't think of a way to bring it back, get her to say what he needed her to say, about everyone starting from the same base line. *Base line, base line. Bass line.*

If he was with them, Rufus, Sam, slender hands girl, right now, would *he* be joining in? No, the beer would have silenced him. He'd be listening to his mind as it picked over the girls, the women, around him, daring him to say something. Anything.

With the can emptied, he felt that softness about his ears that he enjoyed, like the feeling of lying back against the giant pillows Mum reserved for hers and Dad's bed. Not drunk, he was miles from it really, but soft and easy, waiting for real night to descend.

Somebody inside the bar turned the music up an audible notch or two. He hadn't noticed its presence before, and seemingly neither had the gathered people as a handful on the peripheries began to dance, hands jerking, eyes closing. The European students had probably laughed at the scene, the British gaucheness of it; back in Barcelona or Athens or Munich they wouldn't have even left their flats yet. Wouldn't have even finished their food.

And there was a child among them. The boy again. From the north side of the Square, weaving through the crowds, ducking under the arms of dancers and beer-swiggers, quickstepping around ankles so that no one tripped over him, no one noticed him.

But *he* did. High on his balcony, cans at his feet. There was something about the boy's skin, his colouring, his – what was that word? Pallor. He was wan. Words he couldn't even imagine his nana saying. Words her own grandparents might have said. But he was so pale against the skin of those he dodged, a sort of yellow-white, the colour of old shirt armpits. He stood up again, leant over his balcony. Yes, as the boy came closer, he could see his feet, bare, dirty toes beneath those weird pants. The boy was looking for something, someone, he had to be. The way his head snapped from left to right at every junction caused by the arrangement of bodies in the Square, the speed at which his little feet carried him across the stone.

Slapslapslap turn, slapslapslap turn.

He could be on a mission from the estates. A fact-finding mission. Find out what they wear, how they behave. How they handle the prices in the bar. Whether they are planning on moving further in, pushing them out. What their secrets are.

Closer. He leant over. He was directly above the boy now.

If Rufus or Sam had looked up, they would've seen him lurching and he could point and shout, 'A boy! A boy!' until everyone turned to wonder why a barefooted boy was working his way to this block, to stand beneath it and look up.

The boy tipped his head back. Shadows beneath his eyes, around his jawline. Bruising or dirt. Or just shadows. A rip in the narrow flesh of his bottom lip. He wasn't eight or ten. Or twelve, even. He was older. Not a bristle on his chin but his eyes narrowed in knowledge. He was a teenager, but the word didn't seem right for him, conjured bright trainers and affected laughter in shopping precincts. This boy, this youth, was a veteran. The youth raised a hand, fingers darkened with the same bruising or dirt. Or shadow. Was anyone else seeing this? Did anyone else see him on his balcony, straightening up now but leaning towards the youth, letting him know he was listening? Did anyone else see the youth as his other hand began scratching – no, rubbing – at his stomach?

Scuttler.

He couldn't remember Nana saying it, but the word came back to him, sounded in his ears over the bar beats below. Scuttler.

Yes, a local history seminar, some summer school thing he'd taken for extra credits, taught by a local historian. Not seen as the important stuff, but the sepia-tinged fluff for which locals packed out the Central Library and the Portico.

The scuttler's stare prevented him from looking away. His eyeballs were the same old-yellow as his skin, but marbled and ringed with red. The scuttler had seen him. Chosen him. He opened and closed his broken mouth. Both hands rubbed at his belly now. Asking. Demanding something from him, high up on his balcony.

Wait, he mouthed down at the boy. *Wait there.*

He looked about the flat. A pizza box that would rattle with crusts. Plates stacked sink-side, beneath a constellation of cutlery. He opened his cupboard. Tins of beans, chickpeas.

Tubes of puree. What did he eat that a scuttler would? Jules'
cupboard next to the boiler. A box of cereal bars, a spotted
banana. A ghost multipack of crisps. He stuffed the cereal bars
into his armpit, snatched up his keys and walked into his
sliders. The scuttler was waiting for him. Keys in hand, the flat
in darkness, he took the stairs two at a time, the music swelling.

Out in the Square, darker now that he felt the loom of the
tower blocks around him, he smelt the soapiness of the vape
that hadn't reached his balcony. The scuttler had disappeared.
Of course he had. Frightened off by the noise or shooed away
like a pigeon by Rufus or Sam or one of their circle. He looked
up and down the maze paths, shrinking and shifting with
bodies. In the time it had taken to look for food, to get down
to the Square, the scuttler had been swept away, pressed back to
the ginnels and alleyways. He was too late. He stood on the
spot the scuttler had and faced his balcony. Pictured himself
there, the cans at his feet, Jules' fairylights tracing the outline of
the ill-fitting bi-folds behind his camping chair. A bird hide for
humans. They were lucky to get the place. If he and Jules went
elsewhere – and where would he go? Out of the city? Universal
Credit wouldn't make a dint in this rent. He'd probably be
chucked out for claiming it – they would be replaced instantly:
a same-day bidding war after crowded open-house viewings.

The other flats were patient and empty, soft glows from
Ikea table lamps and solar festoons, their inhabitants drinking
and dancing in the Square below.

A lad pushed past, four drinks wedged together in a
lopsided rhombus, a packet of crisps in his mouth.

He heard his name but it was common enough. There
would be others.

But then hands on his shoulders, cheering in his ears:

'Mate!'

'Bro!'

Rufus and Sam, a girl-woman he knew was called Emily.
Beer on breath.

He whirled out from their heavy hands like the scuttler had done. Backtracked on the same stone those bare feet had. Didn't they wear clogs, scuttlers? But the scuttler had gone. No chance to ask him.

He would have a better view from the balcony. He could retrace the scuttler's movements through the people, spot his marbley eyes glinting in the shadows. He could even throw him the food from there, if he didn't want to be approached. What would he say to a scuttler anyway?

The yellow hallway light blinked and stuttered. Doors opened and closed elsewhere. Canned laughter. The flat smelled shut-up despite the open bi-folds, like damp cigarettes though neither of them smoked.

From the balcony, the Square appeared denser with bodies than it had felt on the ground. The boy had been easy to spot with his quick movements, his diminutive height. How sour he had looked compared to everyone else. But he couldn't see him now. The dancing had infected more bodies, the volume had risen further still.

Jules. Her keys on the worktop. 'The door was open. What you doing?'

She took the chair beside him. He felt her eyes moving across his face.

'Solo Saturday night fun,' she filled in. 'A few cans, watching your friends enjoying themselves.'

Out of the corner of his eye, he could see the faded grey cotton sleeve of her *Unknown Pleasures* t-shirt. He had never heard her listen to it, never heard her listen to any music, only the incessant murmur of podcasts from the earbuds that drooped from her collars.

'There's a scuttler,' he said. He intended to add 'knocking about' to offer a kind of nonchalance to the statement but he didn't get round to it.

Did Jules reply? Probably. Maybe she asked him what he meant. But the beats that thudded around the Square had grown louder. Knocked at his temples. Hammered at his ribcage. No families lived in the Square, but for the neighbouring estates, the weekend noise must be a bind. But he had no control over that.

'Yeah. He had bare feet. Said he was hungry.' He raised his voice but it wasn't enough.

'Fancy dress?' he heard Jules say. That would be her interpretation. She had studied economics, extended her student loan to cover a Masters in fashion marketing. Who in their right mind would go to an Ancoats party as a barefooted boy?

'Disappeared in that direction.' He pointed stage right and Jules' head followed his finger. But there was no tea-stained boy, no bare feet.

He had told his mum repeatedly that he and Jules were friends since that's all they had become, in second year it was, but her half-smile and crows' feet at any mention of her name showed she hadn't believed him. His mum spoke too quickly to Jules when she first met her, too enthusiastically, about everything and nothing. She hadn't been to Blackburn, Jules' hometown. 'No. What was it like?' And economics! 'At least that would be useful,' raising an eyebrow at her son. Jules had known exactly how to deal with her, and it had become more natural over the years. But, at her first visit to the flat – solo, his dad feigning overtime – he watched his mum clock their two bedrooms with a drop of her shoulders. Did motherhood mean wishing regular sex for your son?

Had he answered her? He heard cupboards open and close behind him, the desperate suck of the fridge.

'There!' He shot up, threw his hand north-east. A minnow movement. That hair bouncing in then out of view.

It may have been a girl, a woman, dancing. It may have been the miniature schnauzer she clutched to her chest.

Jules didn't care. She hadn't taken local history for extra credits. She probably didn't even know what a scuttler was. She probably had her earbuds in.

He should tell her. Soon he'd be gone.

36

The Cat's Mother

Tom Benn

'LISTEN,' HE SAID —

and dropped the stylus on 'Playboy Short' and Bully sneezed by the door, his collar clicking above a crushed flowerbed of *NME*s, exam revision torn to wet roses.

Henry felt Alice's fingers drumming politely. Her rings playing his ribs as she skinned his socks with a big toe and pushed them off her narrow bed. 'Want your brew?' – peeling her own off the window ledge and blushing under his soft calm stare. Her clippered head showed scalp. A blade of grass in the shell of her ear. When she scratched at it, a snake of tea dripped across the duvet and she spread her toes over the stains, marching to his music in her laddered tights.

'What you reckon?'

'It goes on a bit,' she said.

He tutted; put her brew on the carpet for Bully to lap the dregs.

'He hates blokes,' she said. 'There's only you he won't go for.' They watched Bully nose the empty mug under the bed, then quiet, blinking at Henry with a glazed devotion. Petals of print jewelled the width of his Staffordshire grin. 'Me mam thinks you feeding him steak.'

'Nah. Just likes my music best.'

Alice mawed at her rosary necklace and they kissed for a bit with the beads between her teeth. She smelled to him of Ringos and cider and chain rust from the swings at Painswick Park. 'What we doing tonight?' she said.

'This.'

'Oh. Well, our Jan fancies going pictures.'

'Thought Jan fancied that Tony Kinsella. Or was that you..?'

Alice laughed but it wasn't her laugh.

'…Ever bring him here? Bugsy Malone.'

'Don't be daft. You'd know if I did. You'd hear us.'

They glanced at the shared wall: Siouxsie and Mozza and Marr covering black mould.

'Bloody Tony and his gear,' he said. 'Twat can't tie his Sambas.'

'Bit like you.'

Henry went to kiss her again and she shut her eyes – kohl-rimmed and crusted to soot by Friday late afternoon – but before she could press open his lips he got up instead. She swung for him and missed. He took another record from his schoolbag and put on Pet Shop Boys. 'This the one you were after?'

'I love this.' Alice swayed to it, kneeling on the bed. She smiled when he smiled. 'I never even kissed him, you know. Tony. It was donkey's before *we* did owt.'

'Thought you didn't go for rum lads.'

'Then I best chuck *you*.' She sleeved the single and hugged it.

Someone slapped the shared wall, knocking in threes from the other side. Bully hopped and tried for Mozza's throat.

'Thought you said your dad's working?' Alice said.

'He is.'

'Henry, she's back!'

He put on his shirt and socks, then pocketed his school tie. She offered him his bag. He faced the wall, very still. He heard her trying not to cry but he didn't look. Three more knocks. Bully fretted. Henry turned and she quickly thumbed her wet kohl: 'Want us to come with?'

'Nah.'

'Ring us. If you can.'

Bully barked, barked.

'I think I'm pregnant,' she whispered.

'Shh...'

Bully snapped quiet.

A corner of Siouxsie curled away. The mould began on Henry's side.

'I'll knock,' he said.

★

Next door his mam was filling the fridge with Kwik Save shopping. She wore no shoes, no makeup, a new apricot sundress.

'You been fed, love?'

'Does Dad know you're back?'

'Bet *he's* lost weight and all. The pair of you. Sooner starve than cook a meal.'

Her glass ashtray: back on the kitchen table, dusty from the cupboard.

She stopped unpacking, took her chair and sparked up. 'Ay, what was that racket you were playing first? That poor girl.'

Henry finished putting the food away, then sat and held her hot hands. Five weeks. Neither word nor sight. Now they touched foreheads. She finger-combed his greasy hair, ashing the glass without dropping her eyes, while his stayed monitory, slow blinking.

'Right,' she breathed. 'I'll make us some tea, love.'

★

Henry heard her rattling pots downstairs as he loomed over the burst suitcase sinking his parents' bed. He dug through tangled frocks, bright t-shirts, old knickers, twists of Levis and leggings. The bed springs chinked. He stopped. Slow air churned with dust motes and evening sun. He unzipped an inner pouch: a cut brown envelope of cash. Dividing the notes, a brass front door key for another house. He counted up three-grand. Some notes were splotched a red more blood than pen. Bully began barking next door. Henry put it all back, then went to his own room and listened to Alice worry through the shared wall. He didn't knock.

★

They ate their tea with James Brown live in the boxroom. His dad made space on the table for the Glenmorangie. 'Get the good glasses, Lo.'

'None for me, love.' The phone went but Henry got up first and shut the kitchen door.

'Hello?'

'What you listening to?'

'He's put on *Live at the Apollo*.' From the phone he could spy the Technics speakers pulsing between a mountain range of vinyl soul: Stax, Hi, Federal, Atlantic.

'She's back, then? Happy families?'

'...'

'Can't you talk?'

'Still going pictures?'

'Meeting Jan half seven, but I'm leaving now. Me mam's just let him in.'

'Captain Kipper?'

'They're upstairs. She thinks I've already gone.' Alice giggled. 'He's alright, this one, except for the fishy smell. And he's nice to her. Nicer than Dad.'

'But Bully's not a fan?'

'See you in a bit?'

Henry came back in as the record stopped. Henry Snr spoke with a gobful of mushy peas: 'What's she running up bloody bill for when she bloody lives next door? She's tidy that one, I'm telling you, lad. You've not done bad. But she's a bit bloody keen.'

They heard Bully howl outside, then cackles and moans through the wall, then the back door go: Alice leaving them to it. His dad cupped an ear:

'No wonder the husband buggered off. Be the same story with *this* feller since she can't stop shagging about. They've got her name and number up in the gents' in the Happy Man.'

No soul music. No squeaking cutlery.

Henry's sharp-shouldered mam, exhaling her words like fag smoke in a bright weary rush. 'Far as I know,' she said, 'they're moving to Droylsden with him soon.'

His dad pointed at him with a fork. 'I can see the bloody phone bills now.'

Her voice went chirpy: 'Wonder what the Happy Man has to say about me?'

'Nowt. We're not gossip for this lot round here.'

Acid-bright, goading: 'Such a relief. Finished, love?'

'I'm off.' Henry kneed the table standing too fast. She steadied the whisky.

★

Inside the foyer he stole Alice's elbow and pretended to speed her outside, but she shook him and grinned. There he held her till her softness became a stillness and he felt her smile fall away, his chin itching on the bristle of her shaved head while local lads drifted by and older couples went home.

'Where was she this time?' Alice said.

'He won't ask.'

'Won't *you*?' Scraps of popcorn still starred her chest; her upturned face, trembling and brave as he buttoned her battered denim jacket. 'I'm a fortnight late.'

He popped the Bully-chewed collar. 'You told Jan? She'll think you've been taking notes.'

Jan trotted out of the toilets drying her hands on her white skirt; a white plastic handbag clapped against her hip. 'Ay, I'm not running for a bus in these shoes. Get your boyfriend to nick another car. Mind you, we can't even have the radio on, can we? Not with DJ *Dickhead*.' She relit a Lambert's from her handbag. Alice kissed her cheek, then shared the cig to distract her from the passing cross-chatter and scowls of scented girls leaving with dates – all from the same rival school.

The low sky had emptied. Rushing taxis and Austin Allegros and pavements thick with belted frocks and tashed blokes snaking to the Horse & Farrier. At the corner they caught up with the group from the foyer and Jan gave the best-looking girl a shove and kept going, turning only to see if a lad was watching her arse, which he was, and when the girl yelled: 'Jan Dodds, where you going?' Jan stopped and smoked: 'Don't you worry, love. I've already had him, me! And yours and all.'

But Henry got them across Gatley Road, weaving through night traffic: Jan tottering after Alice; Alice gripping his dry hand, neck turtled in her jacket with fright. They still had to chase the bus. Jan finally threw the fag and carried her heels.

'I need to get pissed,' she panted on the top deck.

'What about your kiddie?' Henry said.

'Me mam's with him. Don't have to be in yet. I don't mean pissed, just, you know–'

'Pissed,' Alice said.

★

They crossed Simonsway and walked down to Portway shops. Only the off-licence was open. Jan pooled their change, elbowing Henry for more shrapnel and dropping a quid in the dark when a young red lurcher shot under the empty moons of the lampposts to sniff out dead cans and crisp packets among the four-foot wildflowers bobbing around the phone box. An old-timer shuffled up the parade and whistled. They passed him their coins and he left them minding the lurcher, off the lead. Alice knelt on the slanting pavestones to hug the dog and ask it human questions and ladder another pair of tights. She got it giddy, squealing under its fretted kisses.

'You're sweeter than our Bully,' she said.

'Well, that's not hard,' Jan said. 'Fucking rabid is your dog,'

Alice struggled to keep it from bolting till Henry crouched with her and stroked it calm. She looked amazed. When the old-timer returned with a quarter bottle in a blue bag Jan snatched it from Henry's fingers and the lurcher woofed and Jan hopped on the spot shaking until the owner whistled the dog away.

They sat on a strip of overgrown grass, watching fights outside the Portway across the empty road. Slaps of skin and bone reached them. Shredded throats competing. Noise to make the quiet seem vast, the estate vast by night, with its echoes and hushed leaf trees.

He caught Alice shivering. 'You cold?'

'Drink up then.' Jan swigged.

'Time is it?' Alice swigged and coughed; he plucked a blue wildflower and tucked it behind her ear.

'Your mam want you in?'

In the pub carpark one bloke was being clawed back by shrieking women.

'Nah. She'll be over there.'

Jan laughed and wiped her chin.

They heard a car engine overrevving before a gold Scirocco bounced the kerb on their side, blocking their view as it scraped to a stop. Broken planks and branches were stacked across the backseats, spoking out of the rolled windows. A red Escort pulled in after it, the stereo rattling the wingmirror. Two Perry Boys got out of the Scirocco in older brother hand-me-downs.

Jan stood the bottle between her thighs to tie up her crimped hair.

When Alice saw the Escort driver she squeezed Henry's hand.

'How are we?' Tony said, winding his window all the way. Jan tried to answer.

Tony killed Bronski Beat. He nodded at them all. 'Alright.' Alice found the flower behind her ear.

'Say hello,' Tony said to the Perry Boys. 'It's bad manners.' His lads said *Iya*.

Henry got a look at him in the driver's seat: a widow's peak and monobrow decked in Freds and Fila, sizing him up likewise. 'What you up to, then?' Tony said.

'Nowt,' Jan said, pressing the bottle onto Henry.

Tony turned to see out the passenger window to the thinning mob outside the Portway: 'Like parents' evening.' Henry clocked his naff earring before Jan rested cleavage on his doorframe. 'How long you had this?'

'Half hour.'

'God, you're as bad as him.'

'Oi,' Tony said. 'Give us a swig on that.'

Henry surrendered the booze and Tony swigged, then gave it to the lads.

'So what you been doing?' Jan said.

'Stopping with me cousin Cid down Violet Court. Been working, haven't I?' Tony grinned and opened his glovebox to show three cash bands curled fat like loo rolls.

'They're not here,' one lad said.

'Who's not here?' Jan said.

'I'm here on business,' Tony said.

Henry buttoned a laugh.

Tony gozzed out the window at Henry's feet. 'Fuck it. They're not coming. Go tell Cid.'

The Perry Boys gave Tony back the bottle.

Tony said to Jan: 'Get in. Having a bonfire at Ringway in a bit.'

'No,' Alice said.

Tony gave her a bold, hard stare. Henry felt her squeeze his hand again. Tony returned the vodka to Henry. 'Mate, she's a right filthy slag, this one. You're a lucky lad.'

The lads laughed into their Scirocco. Jan said something but the engine ate her voice as they tore off.

Tony went: 'Ay, I'm only kidding. But now with that hair anyway she looks like a fucking lez.'

Henry lobbed the bottle and it spidered the windscreen, barely a sound. The driver door opened and he stood taller than Henry and knocked him through Alice and Jan, backward to the shuttered shops, knocking Jan's plastic handbag off her shoulder.

They swung from each other's collars until he tripped Tony and weighted his fall. Tony's jacket lining ripped in his hands and things rained from it and ticked along the ground. Tony got up screaming into his face on a frequency to which Henry's ears were no longer tuned. Tony looked like he had cat fangs.

Behind him, Henry saw Alice cup her ears.

He snatched out the earring, then headbutted him cleanly. Tony knelt in dumb amazement while they all listened to their own racing blood, Tony's washing his front. Then he crabbed for his Escort and stalled before he made off down Ruddpark Road.

Jan prised Alice's hands down and kissed them inside hers. They rocked together on the kerb, waltzing through the booze puddles and windshield shards. Henry was content to be outside himself. His watchful face unmasked. As they danced he picked up Jan's handbag and filled it with Tony's gear, lingering on the final wrap, then dropped it inside with the rest. Jan and Alice fell still. He held out the bag. They both peered inside from far away.

★

Henry waited for Alice to go in and then shut her gate and hopped his own. Lights off. After one. A fag burned in the glass ashtray on the table. A white whisper of smoke to the ceiling. His mam was tipping his dad's Glenmorangie into the sink. Sweat blackened the line of her nightdress. Henry waited for her to glance over her shoulder and then went to bed.

★

She put his brew on the settee arm and put herself between him and a Lizbeth Scott film noir. 'Working with your dad later, love?'

'Half one.'

'That why you pinched bus fare out me purse?'

'I never.'

'Ask.'

She left the house at ten without a word. He dashed upstairs, pulled out her empty suitcase from the wardrobe, concealing a mashed shoebox. He found the cash wrapped in green tissue and counted it again, reboxed it, then raced out.

She was at the bus stop. He hid in Forbuoys and flicked through *Blues & Soul*. The bus came; she queued and got on. He held off, then sprinted over the road. By the time she had a seat on the top deck he was using his clipper card. Back-benched, bottom deck, he unrolled an interview with Kurtis Blow.

A few stops before town she came down with her nose in her handbag, after a cig. She got off and stayed at the stop awhile, cupping her hands to light up. When she crossed he leapt off at the last second and followed her to Hulme, keeping her well ahead. Between them were bikes, prams, old biddies hunched in saris bobbing into the greengrocers, skinny Jamaicans leaning outside a cafe. Graffiti murals on every cladding wall. A line of big lads gave him *fuckoff* stares and he walked in the road to get by.

She turned for an empty passage of loose flagstones and

endless pillars, the wrong side of Princess Parkway, onto a littered common of scorched grass, baby trees in the middle, cutting a corner to knock on the ground floor door of a checkered maisonette. He stepped on her fag butt and waited by a pillar while she knocked again. The clouds split and the flat grey light changed to sunbeams that brought shadow, colour and shape. Nobody came along, just tunes from high windows blasting stuff he didn't know. Sunspots dotted his eyes but he saw her use the brass key to go in.

After ten minutes, she came out puffing another cig and headed back to town alone.

He read the flat number and knocked and waited and spat on the dented door and waited, then looked about before booting it in with three solid kicks, then went inside and shut the broken door with his back. A spray of dry-rot wood patterned the balding carpet. He could smell her smoke. Fish floated in a small tank in front of him: tropical colours, dead over the mini-palm tree and grotto. There was a rotary phone unplugged by the skirting board. A small silver clock on a wonky shelf above. A fly was trapped between the kitchenette windowpane and netting, its wings sawing the silence. Dead cans hid the gas hobs, a spirit bottle pyramid in the sink. A note under the brass key on the countertop. He peeled it from dried lager-spill.

> *I can't give you anything when you're this bad. I told you I always fed the fish.*
> *Lola*

Somebody coughed and his palms soaked. He went for a chopping knife in the sink and the bottle bank clanked into a new array. He edged into the trashed front room, the knife raised, then froze when he saw the woman on the settee, retching a blanket off her chest. She rolled over, quaking and spewing in her sleep. He dropped the knife and opened her gob. Her teeth were sharp, her tongue like another dead fish, the yellows of her eyes showing. He put her on her side and she brought the rest of it up, splashing his shoes. But then she was peaceful and she'd given him her shakes.

'...I love you, Lo,' she whispered, '...Lola, I love you...'

Her sweat stank riper than the vomit. She had on his mam's stud earrings and he took them off, smearing her cheeks and matted afro as he fiddled the backs out. Then he rinsed them under the tap, wiped his shoes, rang 999 and left.

★

Arndale bustle. The indoor market teemed. He zipped past stalls flogging Pisa towers of Betamax; fake City shirts and fox furs; Blitz memorabilia.

'Well, well. Look who's here in time to do half his shift.'

Henry ducked the counter and balled his jacket. Stax vinyl was fanned across the display; tubs sardined with singles. The Dramatics were spinning on the portable player on the back counter, never on loud enough to mither anyone. His dad also kept a pocket radio on for the races, boosting it for the last furlong but otherwise had no trouble listening to both at once. Coined scratch cards were by the radio with a fresh *Evening News.* His dad binned them now, pocketed his mam's quid, and blew the dust. 'What's up with you?'

'Nowt.'

'Then watch the stall while I nip to the bank. Had your dinner?'

'Yeah. Nah. I'm alright.'

'You sound it.' His dad cracked the tillbox and folded a twenty into his shirt pocket and buttoned his Mac. Screaming kiddies chased past with their arms out, playing fighter jets. 'Was your mother in when you left?'

'She went out.'

'Out where?'

'Never said.'

A white feller with orange specs and orange tash flapped through the Motown tubs. A face straight out of *Guess Who?* He read out the sign: *Henry's Soul* and asked if they had any Doris Duke and Henry showed him where to look, while Snr. slipped the Dramatics back into the stacks, then patted his son's arm. 'I'll fetch you some scran. Put on what you want, lad.'

★

'You still not finished them pots?' she said –

and he slotted the last plate in the drying rack, towelled his hands and switched off the cassette radio. He saw her note the quiet: smoking at the table in a house of no music, his dad fed and merry with his winnings, out for the night at the Cock of the North. Then she opened the *Evening News* he'd brought home, tearing the front page when Bully began barking behind the privets. Henry shut the kitchen window.

She said: 'Gunna miss not having your Alice next door, aren't you?'

'We're not talking about it.'

'Me and you, or you and Alice?'

'Both.'

'Don't worry, love. You won't get rid of her that easy.'

He dug the earrings from his jeans; from standing height they ticked into the ashtray. 'I went to the flat,' he said.

'You followed me?'

'I've met her.'

'Saska.'

'Saska?'

She scraped her chair out and slapped him. He coughed with shock. She covered her gob to cry.

'That three grand's Saska's,' his said, his face burning.

She flew out the kitchen. He heard her tumble upstairs and found her knelt by the wardrobe, the shoebox in her lap after counting the money. She looked up when he sat on the end of the bed. 'Money's not mine or hers. It was her brother Troy who hid it at hers a fortnight ago, before he got himself shot dead behind the pub round the corner. Knew some nasty buggers, did Troy. They got who did it quick though. Police come round to tell us.'

'So, you left her again and robbed it.'

'It'll pay for Troy's funeral. Pay for her to sort herself out. I just need to…Look, she's nobody left. They're either dead or in the bloody clink. She'd drink it. And if I stopped with her any longer I would've and all.

'Me and Saska. It's like half the time we're what the other needs; half we're what the other deserves. But I won't have you hating me anymore, love. I'm not having that.'

'Mam–'

'You see the state of her?'

He told her about today, answering her questions when she asked them again, over him, not listening. She was blanched, pacing, pulling on her coat. She rang Saint James', Saint Mary's, the Royal Infirmary, then for a taxi to pick her up at the top of the street and went out to wait.

Henry took the *Evening News* to his room. Ray Dunson's mugshot had been on *Granada Reports* in the week, but Troy's face was new to him. Troy Stewart was Saska's brother. Ray Dunson his alleged killer.

Henry knocked on the shared wall.

★

Bully tugged his lead and towed them to Peel Hall Road, to the park. They let him off on the footbridge over the pond. Alice scattered rips of Mothers Pride over the water and went 'Share!' at the mallards squabbling for crust. She wore her green Oxfam jumper with her Kickers and a bandana scarf; Jan's plastic handbag slung across her chest. Her lippy was Jan's as well.

'Does *your* mam still wallop you?' he said.

'Did the other day when she caught us in her jewellery box.' She examined his bruise in the draining light.

'Last time you lost her old engagement ring.'

'I did.' Her fingers were chalky with makeup, caressing his face.

Henry talked and talked. He told it all twice.

She was shivering without her jacket. 'What is it with mothers?'

He said: 'Least your mam's not a…'

'She might be. I don't go following mine round like Pink Panther.'

'Think it's funny?'

Alice pulled away. 'What, when some bloke gets shot dead? Then his sister nearly dies? You the one ends up ringing ambulance?'

'You forgot the money.'

'You can't leave her be, can you? But she leaves you. It's all she does.'

'And soon you'll have Captain Kipper for a stepdad. Last exam next week. Then you won't even be living round here.'

Alice backed off and turned and left him at the bridge and he whistled for Bully, his collar jingling somewhere in the dark. They caught up to her at the shops. Poundswick lads were leaving the chippy with a ginger girl on a bike, but there was nobody from their year. Alice attached Bully's lead and hooped the handle over a bollard by the chippy. Bully circled it, shortening the rope, his docked tail trying to flutter.

'I'm still late,' she said.

He saw through the golden glass. It was empty, shutting in a minute; but he stopped her from going in and she let him kiss her, Jan's bag pressed between them. 'What's Jan done with that gear?' he said.

'Nowt. Why?' – lifting her face from his shoulder, leaving makeup.

A red Escort skidded to a stop next to them, chart bobbins rattling the windows. The music went off but the engine stayed running. Tony Kinsella jumped out of the back with a Perry Boy from last night. Tony's cousin Cid left the front passenger side while another stayed at the wheel. Cid was Tony but blonder, bigger. Cid said: 'Alright, cunt' and butted him. Bully yanked and scrabbled round the bollard, throttling himself against the lead. Henry, on the flagstones, eyes watering, Bully barking, Alice screaming. When Tony kicked him Alice dived between them but the Perry Boy put her in the back of the Escort and it drove off.

They parted so Henry could see.

'Don't. You. Worry,' Cid told him.

Tony spat on him. Tony pulled a boxcutter and kneed his chest and held the blade to his eye. A blur, tickling his lashes:

'Got till Wednesday to give back the stuff, or we want a fucking grand off you. Dead right.'

Heads turned when the red Escort pulled in again, having looped the parade. Alice fell out, running. She tackled Tony, while Cid played matador with her, swatting her away, laughing. Then they all got back in the car and were gone.

Blinking he saw the chippy lights go off, the sign turned, the staffie arrowed towards him, whining. Alice began to fold herself to hide and cradle him while he shushed her, patting her back as if she were a dog. But when she wiped his eyes he shook off and emptied Jan's handbag over himself: housekeys, tutty, Fruit Salads, Clearblue, heroin wraps.

★

He picked a clapped-out Volvo behind Simonsway, popped the passenger door for her from inside and cuffed glass off the seat. A cassette filled the coin tray: *The Head on the Door*.

'Put it on in a bit,' he said, sniffing back the blood.

Bully twitched between their seats. But it was Alice that

he sensed was about to bolt.

Hunched he lined up a drill bit, hammered it with the brick lump to wreck the ignition lock, his digits rusty and slow, the backs of his hands running with cuts.

'Seen yourself, Henry!' Alice spun the mirror.

'I'm going hospital,' he said. 'We'll go to one in town.'

When the engine started they both jumped.

Alice whispered it, her face glowing in the dashlight, streaked with her kohl and his blood: 'Because you want your mam.'

He shifted Bully to drop the handbrake and reach for her the cassette.

★

The bandana scarf was tie-dyed bloody. 'Looks like a fly,' Alice yawned.

'A dead one.'

She dozed on his shoulder. 'Thems its eyes. Thems its wings.'

Henry crushed up the scarf and returned it to his temple.

At midnight his mam came through and bought a ten pack of Silk Cut from a machine by the reception doors opposite them and gave a cig to a dreadlocked lad with a dishtowel round his ankle and a bag of frozen veg. Henry could feel Alice watching him watching his mother, tipping out her purse for the payphone.

'Mrs Bane. Mrs Bane.' Alice coughed the dry from her voice: 'Lola!'

She dropped the phone and rushed over. 'Oh my God.' Alice moved down one so she could mother him. 'When? Where? Henry, *look* at you! Has nobody-? What happened? How'd you get here?'

'How's your Saska?' he said.

She glanced at Alice. 'They're keeping her in.' She tossed

the scarf onto Alice's lap to touch each bruise, flinching whenever he flinched. 'Who did this to you, love?'

He turned to Alice, who held her tears.

'I'll ring your dad,' his mam said.

He nodded. 'Got you a good excuse now.'

A male voice called her name in singsong Scouse. 'Low-lah...'

Two of them there, tall under the hard glare of the hospital light.

'This the family?' the other said.

'Get stuffed,' she said.

They were bouncer-big, gold chains, Jheri curls, stinking leather coats.

'I'll scream. Think I won't? I'll get you both done.'

They were nodding together, smiling together, a gold canine each.

'So how much was it, Lo?' the Scouser said. His lighter features were pocked with scars and freckles.

'I said I don't know.'

The Scouser's eyes swept Henry, Alice. 'Where's it now?'

'Go. Away.'

'Saska wakes up, do her a favour: you ask her. You listening, Lola?'

Alice held him. His mam held him. Nobody said a word.

He could hear the buzzing silence of the room's wounded strangers, restored by the energy of this listening, till Alice released her breath when the men stalked out through the double entrance doors.

'I need a tissue,' his mam said, sagging when Alice put an arm around her.

'Go with her.' He kept Jan's handbag with him.

Alice mouthed something, but he missed it.

He jogged into the night air, passing Bully tied up. They had reached the carpark beyond the layby. He followed, shouting *Oi*, the cold opening his cuts. They turned when he got close and stood over him. 'It's gear,' he said, opening his fist from the bag. 'Ee-ah. It's worth a grand.'

The Scouser laughed. 'Mad head.'

The other began stag-skulling him, pushing him backward between cars. When the wraps fell, Henry tried picking them up.

'Leave it,' the Scouser said.

'Leave me mam, yeah?' He was lead-boned now with conviction. His stinging eyes stared, didn't float.

★

At hometime Alice was uniformed against the gate in red sunshine, searching the herds headed home. 'Who you waiting for?' he said.

'Jan. We're going Civic.'

Kept-behinds and stragglers from the lower years dripped past gawping at his broken nose and blackeye but he was already used to the stares. Alice bounced off the gate to walk his shadow. Her ears were bare. Cheeks pink from the cold tap.

'You didn't knock on this morning. Thought you'd stay off.'

'Last exam.'

'Henry, I'm so ready for it now.'

'Droylsden. Your mam. Captain bloody Kipper.'

'I didn't mean–'

But then Jan waddled over. 'Absolute minging. Oi, can you even *see* out of that eye?'

'Been waiting ages,' said Alice.

A car horn bibbed and Jan leaned on one leg to better see up the road.

'Don't,' said Alice.

Two leathercoats smoking against a kerbed BMW.

'Right,' Jan said. 'Who the fuck's that and what they doing

over *there* when they should be over here trying their luck with *me*.'

Henry mimed cradling a baby till Jan's easy smile went wire-lipped. But Alice opened his arms and took his hands and he squeezed hers a moment, then gave them his rucksack to mind. The Scouser waved him over. Jan steered Alice away.

★

The Scouser drove past the airport, raced through Heald Green, skipping red lights, overtaking school buses. They chain-smoked in the frontseats with the windows up, the stereo hiccupping dub reggae. The Scouser called the other feller Dee-Dee. Dee-Dee talked along now and again. From under the seat, whenever the Scouser floored it, a tan bullet rolled into Henry's footwell.

They came off a dual carriageway onto redbrick estates, the backstreets mostly Pakistani. A half hour until they stopped on a ghost industrial estate of workshops with bent shutters. Old houses behind them. Henry saw allotments through a razorwire, a dead factory of empty windows hilled above.

Eyes in the rearview: 'Out.'

Nuts and washers shone in cracked cement. An oily van was parked ahead. Two coloured fellers beside it. They watched a blue Daimler reverse in, then Henry's walk up. An enormous white bloke got out of the Daimler in a Crockett shell jacket, grinning, shiny-bald:

'How old are you?'

'Sixteen.'

'What's your name?'

'Henry Bane.'

Dee-Dee clipped Henry's ear. Then the rest jeered and patted him till the white bloke laughed and knuckled his scalp, roughing the back of his school collar.

'I'm White Knowles,' White Knowles said. 'These villains

been alright with you?' The van rocked and barked. 'Well, lads. Best bring them out. Wanna see what me beauties make of him.'

Someone opened the van and three chain-collared Rottweilers leapt down, knocking legs to get to Knowles, who gave them a hard slap each as they climbed him for affection. When it was Henry's turn their barks went deeper, making statues out of all except their master. But Henry stayed crouched. One of them nudged him over, sniffing his face. He patted them all until they lost interest.

'Knew Troy, did you, lad? The brother of that lez. People been saying I had him killed. What you think of that?'

'Ray Dunson killed him.'

'Ray Dunson's one of my lads.'

He saw Dee-Dee, the Scouser, the other two, the dogs.

'Troy wasn't,' he said.

'Smart lad.'

They took the Rottweilers over the wasteground, towards the dead factory where they shot into long grass, chasing birds, rabbits, each other. Knowles clapped when they got nearer the factory yard and his palms boomed and the dogs looked and doubled back.

'Glass up there.' The words prised their way out of his tight jaws while he lit a black Kretek. 'When d'you finish school, Henry?'

'Friday.'

'What you gunna do then?'

'Celebrate.'

'Good lad. Ay, I appreciate the gesture with the gear. Not bad stuff, that. You in business?'

'No.'

'D'you wannabe?' The dogs went after something. 'Who give you the blackeye? We've got you now, son. Any knobheads need sorting, just tell us.' They changed course. 'Wanna look out for your mam, don't you? Tell her not to knock about anymore with cunts like Troy and she'll be sound.' The Kretek danced on his lip. He gestured behind them to his crew, spaced in the grass. 'Listen, keep the money if it turns up. Tide you over till you've picked a life, or a life picks you.'

★

His mam smoothed her frock through the ward, then gripped his arm. She had her hair up and her earrings in. No nattering on the wing: a telly wheeled out for *Albion Market*. She smiled at black nurses engrossed from the desk station and one of them mouthed: *She's awake.*

His mam tugged the bedcurtain to. Sweat had tinted the pillow and linen and her glossy skin gave off the ripe smell. 'They fed you?'

'They've tried.' Saska tilted her head to stare at him awhile, spacey with painkillers, her yellowed eyes wishing, but they wouldn't say for what. 'Does he need a bed and all?'

'He got jumped by a gang of lads.' She dropped the sideguard to perch and Henry sat in a plastic chair. 'I wanted you two to meet, properly.'

'Well? How am I looking? As bad as him?'

His mam leaned away to assess. 'D'you value honesty in a woman?'

Saska smirked, imprisoned: 'Lo?'

'I'll bring Troy's money round but that's it.'

Saska nodded, breathing. They held each other's bones. 'Henry. Open the curtain.'

He did and his mam kicked off her shoes and he turned his chair for the telly. They caught the second half.

★

Alice spilt their brews on the window ledge and then crossed her feet, the duvet laid with paper roses: another dog-shredded *NME*. 'Come here, you.'

Henry switched Schoolly D's 'Saturday Night' for 'Rock the Bells' and she rolled her eyes, then bopped left and right, making the narrow bed squeak. They kissed with her waistband wrinkling his knuckles. He lifted her pullover. She dealt with the bra.

'This new?' he said.

'I've grown.' She tossed it and shed her dusty leggings, springing them at Mozza and Marr, just as his mam's scream came through the wall.

★

He burst home as his mam flung the glass ashtray, his dad ducking into the frontroom as it chipped the doorframe, his dad letting her claw and slap him till he finally slapped her back and then she sat crosskneed on the couch arm, rubbing her face.

'You betted it,' Henry heard himself say –

then his dad's teeth whistle.

'He lost the lot!' she cringed the words.

Henry entered the room but she knocked past and fell upstairs. Creaking floorboards, scraping hangers, the suitcase thump. Bully howled.

His dad scratched his sideburns and paced: 'Your bird's been worried to death, son. Stick with that one. You could do with a bit of bloody sense.'

'Alice?'

They glanced again when the ceiling moved. Heard his mam wail, stamp about. Henry sat where she'd sat and listened for more.

★

A week went –

before the phone rang twice while Henry was testing

carboot finds. First he let it ring, let Irma Thomas finish.

'You never did knock…' Alice said.

Henry listened through the phone.

'…We go tomorrow. Still not packed…'

Then through the shared wall, its spreading mould. 'You've not played owt all week.'

'…Sold me record player.'

He swallowed the quiet. 'He give you a decent price?'

★

Plane engines. Shrouded skies. By Ringway fence Henry smelled the discarded sweetness of cloves, Kretek stubs burning in the moss. A red Escort pulled over where the fence broke onto black fields; the airport flaring beyond from a quarter mile away. Cid Kinsella stepped out first to 'Johnny Come Home' tinny with static. Daimler headlights came on and blinded him. But Henry approached. Let Cid see him.

'Where fuck is it?' Cid said.

Another plane came in low, nearly scraping chimneys, and beneath its wing Cid twigged and ran for the Escort. The night plane went over, whipping through jackets. The dogs had him first. Tony Kinsella got dragged out with the rest, before the plane kissed the runway. Tony tore free across the black grass, dogs chasing him, while Henry went alone and sat in the idling Escort and fed the stereo a cassette from his Harrington. Tony didn't get far.

★

Henry drove their Escort to Violet Court, to the Kinsella cousins' flat, which was sweating by dawn. Woodchip wallpaper greased with fear. The settee piss-stained. A paper lamp gave gentle light, hooded by a bloodwet t-shirt. Empyrean from the tenth-floor window of condensation: a pastel sunrise dyeing the trees and ley arteries and rooftops of the Garden City.

Henry left a breath to weep down the glass and fired up the turntable behind the settee and unsleeved a new seven-inch from a sliding stack: 'Love Comes Quickly'. The stylus fell onto Pet Shop Boys.

Dee-Dee and the Scouser were gone, taking thick rolls of cash and a clingfilmed brick; these men leaving the blurred doors broken or ajar, leaving Henry's shadow to wash the hot sittingroom now, it moving as the sun rose and the needle ran the single to the label. Vinyl popped, a locked groove. Hollowing, unsteady, Henry raised the tone arm of Alice's player and withstood the silence. Then he too was gone. And just his heart and shadow remained, dancing together without music, without a body to case or cast them.

Contents May Vary

Brontë Schiltz

IT WASN'T UNTIL THE third time the fence got kicked in that your mother started to worry. That kind of thing was normal where you lived, and easier to fix than a keyed car, especially since Mr. Brown three doors down was a builder and had been doing you favours ever since your mother defended him that time Mr. Robertson down the road accused him of stealing his garden furniture. Everyone knew that was Mrs. Wilkins next door. In the end, Mrs. Wilkins left the furniture to Mr. Robertson in her will, which even he thought was funny, so that was the end of that.

The third time was different because of the way the wood fell. The first couple of times, you found it in the front garden, and that was okay, that was fine, because that just meant somebody had kicked it in on the way past. The third time, though, you found it splintered all over the pavement, and that meant somebody had come into your garden and kicked it out from the inside, and that was too close for comfort.

Your grandmother had said you should ask the CCTV Man for the footage so that you could catch the person or people who did it, but your mother wouldn't hear of it. The CCTV Man lived on the corner of Birchwood Close, and you couldn't let that lot get involved in your business, broken fence or no broken fence. That was the way things worked around there.

You never went to the police with that sort of thing. Not since they took Tom from number 10 in for questioning when one of the Birchwood lot told them he was acting suspicious when all he was doing was smoking in his own front garden, but when Mrs. Brown called about the brick through her kitchen window, they didn't show up for a week. Margery from number 7 was pleased about that, because she'd always said the police were No Good and now everyone believed her, and she liked being believed.

'We have got to move,' your mother had started saying then. 'We have got to move away from here.'

Your mother told you not to tell anyone you were moving away, and you didn't understand, but you did as she said. You didn't tell Tom or Margery or Mrs. Brown or your best friend Lucy. You didn't even tell your gran. You didn't get a *For Sale* sign in the garden like other people did, and you were excited because you were in on a secret. You left in the middle of the night and drove for hours and hours and hours. It was far too hot by the time the sun was up, but your mother wouldn't let you roll the window down. She was sweating, yesterday's makeup running off her face. She turned on the radio and sang along with songs from before you were born. You knew one or two and sang along as well, and your mother smiled at you and squeezed your hand.

You moved into a flat in Hulme in south Manchester – a tiny flat in a city much bigger than you were used to. The flat came with furniture that smelt like strangers. You felt like you were in somebody else's house, sleeping in somebody else's bed. You still had your special tiger to keep you company, but it wasn't the same. You didn't have a garden anymore, but you had a little balcony where your mother grew herbs to use in her cooking until the boys from the flat opposite started squirting them with stale urine with their water pistols.

You joined your new school halfway through year five, two years after everyone had made their friends. The people spoke differently there and made fun of the way you said *ask* and *dance* and *bath*. You liked the way they said them, but they didn't like you, so you never said so. When you had a supply teacher for English and she asked Jamie to hand the books out and everyone laughed, nobody explained the joke to you. You laughed too so that you didn't feel so left out, and then they laughed at you as well. You asked to go to the toilet and cried in a cubicle like they do in films, and when you went home with bloodshot eyes, you told your mother that you thought you might be coming down with hay fever. You could tell she didn't believe you, but she knew you didn't want to talk about it, so she pretended to.

When you were in year six, your mother found a job in Stretford, so she sent off an application to a secondary school that she could drive you to with only a small detour on her way to work. You got a place there even though you lived outside the catchment area because it was a religious school and your mother's new job had something to do with the Church, and you were relieved because hardly anyone from your junior school would be going there and you'd have a second chance to make some friends.

You were determined to be liked at your new school, so you decided to try to look like the popular girls on TV. On the last day of the summer holidays, you went into your mother's room while she was at Asda and took the tweezers from her makeup bag and sat in front of her mirror and plucked your eyebrows. You were surprised that it hurt and wondered for the first of many times why it was considered so normal for women to injure themselves to make themselves look good.

You persevered anyway, because now you'd started, you thought you may as well finish, but you didn't know what you were doing and plucked much more from one side than the other, then plucked too much from the other side when you tried to even them out and ended up with almost no eyebrows left at all. When your mother got home, you tried and failed to hide your face and she tried not to laugh until she realised how upset you were, and then she didn't have to try. She told you not to worry, and before school the next morning, she spent fifteen minutes carefully drawing your eyebrows back on, and laughed when you said that you looked like the middle-aged lady who lived next door. She plucked your eyebrows for you for years after that. It didn't hurt as much, the way she did it.

Whether it was your pencilled eyebrows or something else, you'd never know, but you made friends just fine at your new school. Your form tutor sat you next to a girl called Anna who showed you photos of her puppy and liked you because you said he was cute. After a week, you started calling her your best friend, because she was your only friend in Manchester and, since you'd lost contact with Lucy, that made her the only person in the world who could answer to that description. The two of you made other friends during your first half-term, too, and when, a few months later, you had to go to the doctors for your HPV vaccine and the nurse talked to you to take your mind off the needle and asked you where you were from, you said 'Hulme' for the first time since you'd moved away from the town where you had grown up.

When you were old enough to go to school by yourself, the tram lines confused you and you somehow ended up on your way to Rochdale and the ticket inspector accused you of fare dodging and you cried in front of everyone. You got off in Oldham and phoned your mother and she met you there and took you out for ice cream. While you ate yours, she called the school and told them you were ill so you didn't get into trouble. She said, 'I can't take you anywhere, can I?' and looked younger than she used to, and you told her you loved her for the first time in years. She cried on the way home.

You were fourteen when you decided you wanted to be an actor. Your drama class went to the Palace Theatre to see *Les Misérables*, which you realised you'd been pronouncing wrong for years, and everyone, even the boys and the teachers, left either crying or laughing that too-loud laugh that people do when they don't want anybody to know that they're really upset. Your teacher told you that it had been running since 1985, and you borrowed a book about it from the library and found out which theatres it had played at and when and tried to work out how many people must have seen and cried over it, but maths was never your strong suit. You knew it was a lot, though, and that was enough. You wanted a job that would make people cry and laugh too loudly and borrow books and attempt maths they couldn't do.

When you told your mother that you were going to be an actor, you expected her to tell you not to be silly, that acting was a job for people who don't have to worry about money, because that's what the mother had said in a book you'd read years ago when her daughter had told her that she wanted to act. Instead, she told you that you'd make a wonderful actor, and you weren't sure if she was saying that because you were fourteen and nobody expects dreams to last when you're that age or if she really meant it, but when you put drama, dance and music down for your GCSE options a few months later, she called you her little star and seemed sincere.

When you were fifteen, people from colleges came to give talks at your school and what they said about employability made you nervous, and you began to understand why the mother in that book had said what she did and wondered why your mother hadn't said the same. When you started sending off your applications and had to choose your options, you put down French and psychology along with drama and music, because they were Real Subjects that would help you to get a Real Job if acting didn't work out. Your own pragmatism irritated you, because you were determined for it to work out and it seemed pathetic to start to give up on a dream that you hadn't even had for a year, but that was life, whatever that means.

In your first year at college, you turned around in the lunch queue and knocked your food all over a girl two inches taller than you. You paid for her food to apologise, and she sat with you because you were wearing a *Fight Club* t-shirt and *Fight Club* was her favourite film. You didn't tell her that it was an old top of your mother's and that you'd never actually seen *Fight Club*. You pretended to know who Marla Singer was and agreed with her opinions. She invited you out for coffee on Friday after your classes had finished and you said yes. She was very pretty.

You watched *Fight Club* when you got home and decided you didn't agree with all her opinions after all. It annoyed you that you'd missed the chance to debate with her, because she was passionate and clever, and you wanted to know how she argued. You met her on Friday and argued about the government instead. You pretended to understand what she was talking about, and she laughed and told you that she studied politics, and you said that she was cheating.

The first time she said 'I love you,' it reminded you of your mother. She said it too fiercely, as if you needed one another to survive. You thought of when your mother would say, 'Girls need to stick together,' and you would say, 'Yes', but think, *why?* There were girls you didn't like, girls you hated. You didn't want to stick with them. You told her that you loved her too a week later as she licked strawberry milkshake from her upper lip in a café near Manchester Cathedral, and she looked too happy and you wondered if you meant it.

She was really very very pretty.

She invited you to her house and you went because she lived in Didsbury and you wanted to know how much money she had, and it was impolite to ask even though you knew she would have told you. It really didn't matter to you, but your mother hated people with money and that made you curious. You rang the doorbell, and she opened the door and kissed you before she let you in. She took your hand after you'd taken off your shoes and you went upstairs to her room. Her walls were covered in pictures of Joan Jett.

'That's Joan Jett. She's from the seventies and eighties,' she said when she saw you looking at them.

You didn't tell her that you already knew who she was. Instead, you asked if she was still alive.

'Oh yeah,' she said. 'I saw her at Lancashire County Cricket Ground last year. Would you like to see the photos?'

She didn't wait for you to answer, she just knelt down and took an A4 envelope out of a drawer at the bottom of her badly painted bedside table while you wondered why somebody born in the fifties and still alive today was *from the seventies and eighties*, and if you were *from* the decades in which people cared the most about you, and what decades you'd be from. You hoped that it wouldn't be the nineties or noughties, because then you really wouldn't have done very well.

She sat down on her bed and patted the space next to her. You sat down beside her, your thighs touching. Hers were firmer than you were expecting, and you wondered if she was sporty. You reached out to take the envelope and she pulled it back.

'Only touch the edges,' she said. You must have looked surprised, because she added, 'Sorry, I just don't want them to get smudged.'

'That's alright. Do you want to hold onto them?' you asked, already knowing that she did. She smiled, and reverently leafed through them.

'She's still pretty,' you said.

'She's beautiful,' she said, which either made you jealous or feel that you ought to be.

When you got home, you told your mother that you were

in love with a rich girl just to see what she'd say. She shook her head but said that all she wanted was for you to be happy, and you went to bed slightly disappointed. You almost wished that your mother didn't love you so much more than she hated money, because you liked people with strong opinions.

You and your girlfriend broke up two months later after she stayed at your flat and you came back from the bathroom to find her tidying the lounge. You messed it up again after she left. You and your mother had always been messy people, and that was fine, perfectly fine.

When you were eighteen, you came home to find your mother in tears over a bill she couldn't pay. She told you not to worry, but of course you did. The next evening, you went out and applied for a job at a pub off Oxford Road so that you could do something to help. You spent hours writing up a CV before you went, but the manager barely looked at it. He just looked you up and down in a way that reminded you of how the farmers look at their cows on *Countryfile*, then offered you the job. He stood too close to you and touched you too often when he taught you how to serve drinks, and you knew exactly why he'd hired you, but a job was a job, as your mother used to say.

Your contract began the following week. You wore the revealing uniform and smiled when men three times your age told you to and didn't complain when they dropped their money over the bar so that you'd have to bend over to pick it up or slipped fivers into your bra and waistband, because as the weeks went by, your mother stopped crying and started sleeping again, and that was all that mattered.

You were afraid of ending up like your mother, and even more afraid of her spending the rest of her life like that, so you decided to grow up and accept once and for all that you were never really going to be an actor and to study French at university instead, consoling yourself that at least you could write your dissertation on *Les Misérables*, about which you were then pretty sure you had memorised enough pointless facts to do very well on the specialist round of *Mastermind*.

Your mother wouldn't hear of it. You told her that you were giving up because you loved her. She told you that it didn't work like that. You applied to Manchester School of Acting, and your mother drove you to your audition and you sang 'On My Own'. Your mother came into your room with jam around her mouth holding a letter with the MSA insignia on the envelope a few months later. When you told her that you'd been accepted, she went out and bought the only bottle of champagne you'd ever seen in your home other than the ones that your gran used to bring at Christmas. So that was that.

When you were in your second year, you went out in the Northern Quarter with a group of friends and bought the first round because you'd just heard that you'd got a small theatre role you'd auditioned for a few weeks back and wanted to celebrate. The woman in front of you had hair exactly like another of your friends, and you presumed it was her and said, 'Alright, fuck off so I can get my drinks.' When she turned around and you realised that she was a stranger, you apologised at least six times, but she laughed and said that it was alright, and when you went back to your friends, you didn't tell them what had happened because you knew that they'd laugh, and you didn't want her to think that they were laughing at her.

About three-quarters of an hour and several drinks later, 'Hanging On The Telephone' came on and you tried to convince your friends to come and dance with you, but they said that they weren't drunk enough to make idiots of themselves just yet, so you went by yourself because it was one of your mother's favourite songs and had been your absolute favourite for as long as you could remember, and not to dance to it felt like blasphemy.

You stood with your back to the rest of the people on the

dancefloor so you could lip sync at your friends and tripped over your own feet and stumbled backwards into the same woman you'd accidentally insulted earlier, and when you turned around to apologise, she said, 'We've got to stop meeting like this.'

You said, 'This is my favourite song!' because you couldn't think of anything more appropriate, and when she said, 'Me too!' you instantly fell more in love with her than you had ever been with your rich college girlfriend. You danced and sang along together, and she wrinkled her nose and curled her lips as she growled the 'oh's, and you kissed her as soon as the song finished because it seemed the only thing to do, and your friends whistled and weren't surprised when you grabbed your coat and bag and left with your arm around the other woman's waist before you'd even been at the bar an hour.

Your recollection of precisely what happened after that was a rosy haze by the time you woke up just after six the next morning with her arm draped across your chest. You wished that someone had told you whether or not it was impolite to move your one-night-stand's limbs so that you could use their loo. You deliberated for five minutes, looking at the woman beside you and wondering how she could sleep so peacefully with the sun shining so brightly onto such pale eyelids, until you decided that it was creepy to watch her sleep and that it would be more impolite to wet yourself in her bed, and then you shifted out from under her arm and stumbled around her corridor until you found her bathroom. When you came back, she was still asleep and you were going to be late for a rehearsal if you didn't leave soon, so you got dressed and wrote your name and phone number on a post-it note on her desk and left her sleeping.

She called you nine days later, after you'd convinced yourself that she just wasn't as interested in you as you were in her and that was a shame but you'd get by, and told you that the Star and Garter was putting on a Blondie night and asked if you'd be her date. 'I bet you say that to all the girls,' you said, and she laughed a sort of somehow decorative laugh that you suspected was reserved for people who she didn't know well but wanted to. Before she hung up, she told you that her name was Eva and you laughed at yourself for having convinced yourself at the bar that you were in love with someone whose name you didn't even know.

'What?' she said.

'Nothing,' you said. 'It's a lovely name. Eva.'

You spent the evening digging through your drawers to find the most Debbie Harry clothes you owned and settled on a pair of jeans with a slightly higher waistband than the rest and a jacket that had always been a bit too big for you and smudged pink lipstick over your cheekbones for blusher. When you arrived at the pub, you realised that you were the only person who had dressed up, and you were trying to decide whether to go home and get changed or not when Eva arrived looking like she'd walked straight out of 1978, and then you couldn't decide whether to be more embarrassed that you'd dressed up or that you'd not dressed up impressively enough. You both laughed at yourselves and each other, and when she touched up her lipstick after she kissed you, you wondered if she was always a perfectionist or if her attention to detail was reserved for Blondie-related circumstances and decided that you liked her for it either way.

She sang the French parts of 'Denis' and 'Sunday Girl' perfectly and you asked her if she was fluent, and she said that her mother was French and that she had grown up in a village just south of Calais. You told her that you'd always wanted to go to France, and she said that the two of you should go together, and you thought she was joking until a plane ticket with your name printed on it landed on your doormat a few weeks later while you were getting the fluff out of the washing machine filter. You left it there because picking it up felt like a commitment, and you didn't know how to tell her that you couldn't afford to go to France. She called you a few hours later and said 'Well?' instead of *hello*, and you could hear that she was smiling.

'How much is it?' you said before you could stop yourself.

'Free, for you. It's a gift,' she said.

'You really didn't have to,' you said.

'I know,' she said.

When you came home from France feeling slightly less linguistically competent than you had before you left, Eva asked you to move in with her, and you said yes and didn't care about how fast things were moving or that it would be inconvenient for your housemates to find someone else to fill your room. Eva's Ancoats flat overlooked the canal, facing east towards the Etihad and the morning sun, and when your mother came to visit, she said that she hadn't realised Manchester could look so beautiful, and you felt that it was her way of telling you that she thought Eva an excellent choice.

You'd never been the type, as a child, to dream about your future wedding, mostly because you never thought you'd have one, but one balmy August morning, as you walked around the marina, you asked Eva to marry you just because you could. You expected her to say no because she usually hated traditions purely on principle. She wouldn't even let you put fairy lights around the windows at Christmas or buy her chocolate at Easter. When she said, 'Well, since you asked so nicely,' you said, 'How on earth are we going to afford a wedding?' and she quoted you on Facebook when she changed your relationship status to *Engaged*.

You got married a couple of years later, when you had saved up enough for a service at a three-star hotel near Piccadilly Gardens. Your gran came up from Kent to be there and didn't say anything about having hoped for great-grandchildren. You asked the DJ to play 'Hanging On The Telephone' for your first dance, and this time, Eva didn't bother to fix her lipstick after she kissed you.

It was just after your twenty-ninth birthday that the

headaches started. Eva ignored you when you complained about them at first, because you liked complaining. You complained about the weather and noisy neighbours and people who ate with their mouths open at restaurants and the fact that insects fly against the same window over and over again when another is clearly open and the inconsistent characterisation of Inspector Morse. The headaches seemed to be just another addition to the ever-expanding list of things you liked to moan about while Eva did her makeup or made you both a cup of tea. It wasn't until you woke her up in the middle of the night rummaging for paracetamol in her bedside table that she suggested you visit a doctor. You resisted, but she was insistent.

'It's probably nothing, but it's best to be on the safe side,' she had said, but you could feel her uncertainty in the way she covered your hand with her own as she passed you a cup of tea. She offered to go with you, but you said, 'No, I'm not a child,' and meant, *No, there might be something wrong and if there is I want you to hear it from me.* You told yourself that you were just being neurotic, but that wasn't like you. The doctor was around your age, which reassured you for a few seconds because it felt almost like meeting a friend for coffee, except that there was no coffee, and the room smelt unappetisingly of antibacterial products, and friends don't ask, 'What can I do for you today?'

You told her about the headaches, and she asked you if they made you feel nauseous, and if you'd been feeling drowsy recently, and if you'd noticed any deterioration in your eyesight, and you answered yes to everything and didn't want to think about what that might mean. She told you that she was referring you to a specialist at the Salford Royal, but not to worry, it could be nothing. She didn't say what kind of specialist. She didn't have to. When you got home, you told Eva that everything was fine.

You were put on a two-week waiting list. During that

time, you said nothing to Eva and found excuses of varying degrees of convincingness for your constant restlessness, telling yourself that it would all be alright, you had nothing to worry about. Cancer was something that happened to other people, not to you.

You went to your appointment while Eva was at work, taking the 33 even though the woman who had booked you in had advised getting a lift, and when the radiologic technologist noticed your wedding ring and asked if your husband had come with you, you just said, 'Wife,' and didn't tell him that she didn't even know you were there.

When the results of the scan came back and a kind-faced doctor invited you into her office and leaned forwards in her chair, speaking in hushed tones, you knew what she was going to say before she said it. You asked if you were going to die, and she said not necessarily, that there were options, the best being surgery, but that there were risks attached. You said that you didn't care. You were a daughter, an actor, a wife. You were much too young to die.

You finally told Eva when you got home, the words spilling out between sobs that had been building for hours, and she held you and stroked your hair and said, 'It's okay, it's okay,' even though you both knew that it was a lie.

On 6th October 2019, you underwent neurosurgery intended to save your life.

On 7th October 2019, you woke up without it.

The surgeon told Eva that your temporal lobe had been damaged during the procedure, and that while they couldn't rule out the possibility of recovery, your long-term memory may have been irreparably damaged. Eva repeated this to you when you drifted out of unconsciousness and asked for your mother for the fifth time that morning.

You remember none of this.

Rats and Mice

Mike Duff

So I'm walkin down Miller Street headin toward Victoria Station. I've had a drink an it's getting late. I notice a figure swayin in front of me. I recognise immediately the United shirt (it's one of them green an yella ones brought out to commemorate the centenary an Newton Heath's part in it). I fuckin hate Newton Heath, fuckin smackheads an women with 'honey I shrunk the giro' kinda faces.

As I get alongside him our eyes meet. I look away but he's seen me.

'Fuck me with a wooden broomstick an call it the brush off, if it aint me old mate Bobby Doyle,' he says in a drunken slurred Welsh voice.

'Right Bernie,' I say, 'where you off?'

A gleam comes into his eye an he offers me a can of Stella. 'Not seen you for a long time Senor. Off to the Press Club, you wanna come?'

An I notice the Welsh voice has mellowed to near Mancunian after 30 years in the City. Quite a few of them spent in Strangeways an other of Her Majesty's guesthouses.

We walk along together. It's maybe half two in the mornin.

An me mind gets lost in useless thought as the tangents of

time take over an I think about the first time I saw Bernie. We were on a train headin for Victoria Station, just like now, both aged about fourteen. We'd bin to Blackpool. Davis was with a gang of Miles Plattin lads an I was with me cousin Rafferty. Rafferty knew them all so no hassle.

It was a good laugh at first, flingin light bulbs an toilet rolls out of windows, an other kids stuff. The train was one of them old sorts that had a corridor that ran right down the side of the train an you could swap compartments at will. No ticket collector on. So no authority figure to safeguard the interests of Mr. Commuter.

Anyway the train stops at Preston an this suited man gets on. Our compartment is full so he settles down in one about four away. Ten minutes pass by an we get bored. There's a little Livingstone in even the youngest Mancunian so we go explore. There's a girl with a good size pair of tits in one carriage but her boyfriends with her an he's built like Jean Claude Van Damne on steroids, so we leave them well alone.

We move a little farther down an we come across Mr. Suit, an he's chosen to be alone.

'Never mind, we'll relieve the boredom,' says Davis, who is firmly in charge.

An we all pile in.

'These seats taken?' says Rafferty as he climbs on the luggage rack.

The little shithouse. No chance of gettin punched up there. Our host moves a few things for his uninvited guests, puts them in a briefcase, an then commits suicide by speakin.

'No you're alright,' he says.

An I wince; he's got a Scouse accent, a posh one but Scouse nonetheless. There's a stunned silence at our end, we've caught an enemy spy. 'Hey who'd you support, our kid?' says Rafferty as Bernie blocks the door.

Now Mr. Suit is in a quandary an I don't mean one of them places where you mine stone.

He can't say United cos of his accent, he can't say Liverpool or Everton, he must know enough to know that, an he'll get beat to fuck if he says he don't follow the beautiful game. I've gotta say at this point I was sorta enjoyin meself, dint think it would go much further, just a bit of fun. Me Mam had always kept me away from Rafferty an his crew, she said they were accidents waitin to happen. The Scouse lad is silent. He's roughly twenty but Bernie, although a kid, could do him anytime an that's without the others helpin, which of course they would.

Bernie decides to put the Scouser at ease.

'Don't matter to us. It's your business.'

An the Welsh accent gives the Scouser a little confidence cos he says

'Liverpool.'

An I think a young Charles Bronson must be in the next carriage cos this is where he got the idea for the *Death Wish* films from.

Rafferty perched on the luggage racks begins to sing.

'In the Liverpool slums

In the Liverpool slums

They go to the dustbin for something to eat

They find a dead rat an they think it's a treat

In the Liverpool slums'

The Scouser laughs a nervous laugh. Rafferty takes over the questionin.

'Wot's your name our kid?'

'Richard,' says the sweatin Scouser.

'Yeah, you look like a Dick,' says Rafferty, milkin the laughter. 'Second I seen you I thought that man is a Dick.'

Bernie don't like the loss of attention.

'Like your briefcase,' he says, 'could do with one for me exams. Can I have it?'

Point of no return time, Richard has to fight or try to cut an run, but he decides to do neither. Bernie empties the contents of the case over him an says, 'Ain't really got no exams, but I can use this in a blaggin. Then when the Filth fingerprint it they'll arrest you, cos you're a Scouser.'

We all laugh.

Richard by now is starin out the window.

I can see it's gone too far, the man is shakin in fear. If he was braver, he'd get the beatin done with, just butt Johnny Wright by the door an see wot happens.

He makes a serious mistake. He gets up slowly to leave. We're nowhere near a station so he's just bein yella.

Bernie grabs him by the throat an throws him down, I never expected none of this.

Rafferty shouts: 'See as he got any money to lend us, Bernie.'

The Scouser starts cryin. He's bleedin while swimming amongst piranhas.

'I hate to see a man cry. So shut up,' says Bernie.

There's a horrible silence, filled only with the sound of Bernie goin through Richard's pockets. The final act of humiliation comes when Bernie strips him of his watch an passes it to Rafferty.

The train pulls into Salford, next stop Victoria Manchester, the game is reachin its climax an Richard's only hope is Jean Claude gettin off an us goin to mither Big Tits. But reality is a bitch cos the train choo-choos out of Salford with the carriage line-up intact.

I know wot is happenin is wrong but I ain't got the bottle to stop it. Don't get me wrong I ain't like Rafferty, I ain't frightened of none of them, includin Bernie. It's just sometimes easier to be one of the boys. So I look on fascinated.

'Now,' says Bernie, 'we're gonna play a little game.'

As he's sayin it he pulls out of his pocket a dice. The poor Scouse is mesmerised. Let's have it right he's willingly given up his money, his watch, his briefcase an his self respect.

'Know wot the game is?'

The Scouser shakes his head an I'm prayin the train pulls into Victoria an the game gets postponed an never replayed in Liverpool with me cast in the part of Richard. Though if it did some fucker as well as me would get well an truly hurt.

'Right, here's the rules, explain them Rafferty.'

Rafferty sits up on the luggage rack, as best he can, his head against the train roof.

'Right, a dice as you know is numbered one to six. In our little game you get to roll it an if it comes up one, two, three, four or five we kick your Scouse head in, Dick.'

Twat, I'm thinking. Rafferty ain't never kicked no fucker's head in ever.

Bernie takes over speakin. His face is a foot away from the Scouser an his eyes are mad.

'You're probably wonderin wot happens if it comes up six,' he says.

The Scouser is terrified. In his fear he's both smilin an cryin.

'If it comes up six then you get to roll a fuckin again,' says Rafferty.

Everyone is laughin, everyone except Dick an me. I decide to end the game. No more humiliation, no rollin no dice. I take the Scouser out with one punch to the jaw. He falls sparkled. Everyone looks at me gobsmacked.

We get off the train as fast as possible, an for all the wrong reasons I'm immediately one of the gang. Bernie is full of admiration.

'Wot's your name?' he says.

'Bobby Doyle,' I say.

An the clock ticks forward again as we stand outside Victoria Station.

'You comin to the Press Club then?' he says.

'No,' I say, 'got work in the mornin.'

An we go our separate ways.

The Headteacher

Okechukwu Nzelu

FOOD ALWAYS TASTES BETTER stolen. The thought went back and forth in Jeremy's mind as he watched the sausage rolls, as keenly as if they might somehow move or transmute. Hiding in the spare room while the party carried on downstairs, he ran through myths about food and calories. Party food doesn't count. Nobody would see him eat them, so it wouldn't count. But he would know. And when his stomach started to swell, his husband would know. When his arse sagged, and his chest drooped. He should never have accepted them from that man at the door. What was his name? Nathan? Something like that.

Jeremy had been in such a good mood just before he let Nathan in, too. Even after he saw the plate of what was probably leftovers in the young man's hand, he'd tried to smile. He'd even said he would hand the sausage rolls round at the party. But then Nathan had made that bizarre joke about bringing sausages to a party hosted by two gay men, and he'd laughed that braying laugh and showed his uneven little teeth, and something had snapped, or slipped in Jeremy's mind, and that was that. He'd grabbed them, made his excuses, and now he was here, staring down a plate of sausage rolls while people ate and drank downstairs.

Why would anybody bring sausage rolls to a party at a

house like theirs, in a neighbourhood like this? Hadn't Nathan seen the brand-new paint on the door, sixty quid a tin? Hadn't he seen the plantation shutters? Granted, it had only been a few weeks since Jeremy and Matthew had moved to Altrincham. And Matthew did like to point out that it was the smallest house on the street, dwarfed on either side by properties with more bedrooms than leaves of neatly mown grass. But all the same, this was a step up the ladder. There was a barrister two doors down. Across the road, someone from a Netflix drama. Jeremy looked at the sausages. What would the neighbours think if they saw him eating these? Did the people on Cameron Street even go to bakery chains? It seemed unlikely.

He should have got rid of them immediately. He had thought about throwing them away, or pretending to trip over and tipping them artfully to the floor. But what if Matthew saw them in the bin? What if they stuck to the plate when Jeremy faked falling over, and he had to shake them off? Besides, it would be fun to say something almost kind about the ways in which they didn't quite pass muster. He tried to remember the details of the offending remark, but Nathan had fumbled it halfway through and it hadn't all been audible. He'd clearly been expecting Matthew to open the door. Matthew would have been much more hospitable than his husband to that tawdry little attempt at humour, especially from an ex-pupil. Jeremy had just given him a look and told him where to hang his coat.

In the spare room, he rolled his eyes and wiped his mouth. Sex-starved straight men have a way of bringing this sort of smut into every context where it is least welcome. And they always seem to think their gay jokes are *original*, the first and best that have ever been made. Jeremy thought what it would be like to bite down hard and feel himself symbolically avenged.

Yes, that was enough. Just the thought of it was almost as

good. He would have to leave the spare room soon, anyway. In a minute, he'd have to go down to the party and take the sausage rolls with him. Nathan would still be standing around with the other ex-pupils, and the other teachers. Jeremy groaned inwardly. Public sector workers are fine in small numbers, and some are even good conversation - civil servants, for example, who tend to either have gossip on cabinet ministers, or stay quiet because they already know that nobody cares what they do with bins all day. Doctors you can talk to, as they often have more than a hint of a desire to privatise the whole thing. Teachers, however - overworked, underpaid, undersexed - are the worst. All of them so tightly wrapped up in their little worlds that they can't think of anything interesting to say. Like nurses, with their tired, over-washed uniforms and near-identical anecdotes about their sad little staycations.

Jeremy had measured out his life in *mmm*s and tight, grudging smiles. Teachers always had another anecdote, another in-joke that only *those* staff at *that* school would ever understand. Funny how every teacher is the hero of their own story. Even if they seem like they're making fun of themselves, they're really trying to tell everyone how cute and funny and humble they are. None of them are talking about the fact they failed in every other job but this one, or how they saw Mr Peters fondling little Jimmy after PE and didn't say a word.

Jeremy took a quick look in the mirror. He practised the expression - bland, unconcerned - that he would present to the room when he came downstairs with a tray of baked goods that was every bit as full as it had been when Nathan had arrived. He would make up some excuse and smile as though he hadn't even thought about eating them all, one by one or all at once. He should have been an actor.

He'd had enough practice. He'd played the therapist when, years ago, Matthew told him the school trip budget had been cut again. He'd pretended not to mind about Matthew's late nights, his early mornings, the pay so low it barely reached ankle height on Jeremy's. He'd listened gently to Matthew's accounts of the abuse – verbal and, once every couple of years, physical – that Matthew received from students, and occasionally parents too. He'd smiled at all the work Matthew did during his 'vacations'. He'd been a consummate mime when Matthew told him the board had appointed that bald little oaf Karl Moore to be the Head, despite multiple rumours that he'd tried it on with half the women in the staffroom, bad toupee apparently notwithstanding.

Acting wasn't the hard part. That was mostly just listening. The difficult thing was being married to someone who cared enough about ordinary children that he cried when they couldn't go on school trips because the Head had spent the money on a hotel room for his mistress. What kind of man cared so much about people who weren't family, weren't even colleagues, really? Matthew had been like that when they first met, but Jeremy had never thought it would last. It had lasted their whole marriage, Matthew beloved of everyone and Jeremy, not quite as handsome, nowhere near as kind.

It only got worse with time. Twenty years ago, Karl had finally been sacked. Jeremy wished he could have been there to see the little pig in a wig escorted off the premises, but he'd been at home at his computer when Jeremy came back with the news. Jeremy had listened patiently. And then he'd had an idea.

'Maybe it's time for you to leave too,' he'd said.

Matthew'd scrunched his face up. 'What? Why?'

'That Academy's a bit of a sinking ship isn't it? Even before Karl, there was that budget problem, and the Ofsted reports, and all those staff leaving every year. Now this.'

Matthew gave a tiny nod. Jeremy pressed his advantage.

'What's the point wasting more of your career in a place like that? There are other jobs.'

'Nice to know you think I've been wasting my career,'

Matthew said, quietly.

'Teachers leave schools all the time. Most people in your position would have left years ago. And you could do anything you want.'

'I'm thirty-five,' Matthew'd said. But he'd said it in the way all men say it when they approach middle age: part statement, part question.

'Thirty-five is young,' Jeremy responded. 'There are other things you could be doing. Maybe Karl getting sacked is a sign from the universe.'

Matthew'd actually seemed to think about that one for a moment, but when he eventually spoke he declined the idea. 'I can't leave now. If I handed in my notice right after Karl got sacked it'd look like I support him and I'd never get a decent reference. Let me think about it.'

Jeremy had let the matter drop. He'd made his point. He assumed that further thought on Matthew's part would lead him to a more sensible course of action, not less. What was Matthew doing in a school like that, anyway? Granted, Matthew hadn't had as much money as Jeremy, growing up. He'd only gone to a mid-table private school in Cheshire, not even boarded like Jeremy had, down in Oxfordshire. Still, that life had never been right for Matthew. He'd never known anything like these children's lives, no heating in the home, parents working all hours for no money, every other child on free school meals. When Karl was sacked, Jeremy had thought Matthew would finally come to his senses.

But then Matthew applied for Acting Head in a matter of days. And once that school had gotten their claws into him, they were never going to let him go without a fight.

Jeremy grabbed the tray of sausage rolls, opened the bedroom door and stuck his head out, sampling the noise from the party before he committed himself to re-entering it. The sounds of conversation bubbled up the stairs to him, with the occasional voice identifying itself. There must be nearly a hundred people in the lounge, treading their biscuit crumbs into the carpet. And Jeremy had agreed to put up with it, for Matthew's sake of course. Jeremy understood the need for a state school system, and he looked on with some sympathy at Matthew's desire to be a part of it. He had, however, expressed some reservations about inviting their education system, seemingly in its entirety, into their house for drinks. The only reason Jeremy consented to hosting Matthew's colleagues and some of his former students from the Academy - and consented to it taking place in their own home, where the LVT had just been laid down in the hallway - was because this was the last time he would have to see any of them. After 35 years spent working in that school and 34 years of Jeremy wishing he would get another job, his husband was retiring. It had been tough convincing Matthew to leave while he was 55 and still had some life in him. He'd only just turned the school around. If it hadn't been for the rental income from the new flats in town, he'd probably have stayed until he was 60.

The party had been going for a full hour and the guests had swarmed through, into the dining room and the conservatory. Someone had taken over the smart speakers, ousted Jeremy's calming classical-contemporary playlist and replaced it with their own choice of music. As he descended the staircase, someone was whining about a wonder wall.

He stood in the hallway behind the glass doors to the lounge. He took a deep breath and opened it.

On the other side of the door, a woman with green eyeshadow turned to him. There was a kind of default smile on her face that faded momentarily as she recognised him and walked over.

'Jeremy,' she said. 'So good to see you.'

'Mrs Parkinson,' he smiled. 'So glad you could make it.'

'Call me Susan,' she said. Jeremy nodded and made a mental note not to. Once, he'd called her 'Parkers', which she'd hated because she said it made her sound like someone who went beagling. He'd blinked at her a couple of times before he realised that this was an insult, but by then the conversation had already moved on.

'Where's Matthew?' he asked her.

'Don't know,' she said, blithely making no effort to look for him. 'Probably off somewhere being adored. You want a drink with those?' She nodded to the tray of sausage rolls that Jeremy had forgotten he was holding. Reddening slightly, he set them down on a nearby table and picked up a glass of the ice-cold, bone-dry Pecorino he'd had recommended by last week's wine guide. He would mention it to Mrs P at some point, knowing she'd have no idea what it was. And she'd keep her face frozen still, determined not to admit any ignorance in front of him.

'Much better,' she said, a little too kindly, as though she'd just supervised the de-lousing of a child. 'Alright, then. What shall we drink to?'

'I'd like to drink to *you*,' said Jeremy, watching her carefully. But she barely raised an eyebrow.

'Me?'

'Absolutely. Nobody has been more supportive of my husband than you.'

She eyed him for a moment. 'That's true.' She raised her glass, took an approving sip and, making no excuses, went off in search of better company.

Jeremy was not terribly sorry to miss out on more conversation with her. He knew all about Mrs P. She'd been the one to get her claws into Matthew first, making him practise his Teacher Voice until it was perfect. She'd shown him how many slides he could cut out of his PowerPoints in order to make the best use of lesson time. She told him which members of the leadership team to steer clear of after the weekly meetings, and which extracurriculars to avoid if he wanted to keep his Saturday mornings free. Such a lot of energy to expend on someone totally unrelated to her. The truth is, she'd groomed him for leadership from the start. She told him how to keep the difficult staff on side; how to handle Mr Green's moody outbursts after the awful Year 9 class he always taught last thing on a Monday; what to buy Mrs Jones for Christmas so she'd lend a hand with classroom displays all year; which seat in the staffroom was only for the Head. It amounted to a kind of informal internship. It must have added hours to her working week.

Jeremy hadn't minded so much at first. It meant more money. They'd gone to Rome with his Head of Department raise. That hotel with two sinks in the bathroom. And on those first few mornings in the role, Jeremy had felt a kind of pride watching his husband set off for work, his suit pressed, his shirts starched, his hair gelled, ready to educate the community (not *their* community, of course). He'd still felt Matthew was his, then, however long he stayed away. But it didn't last. It was Mrs P who had convinced Matthew to apply for promotion after promotion.

What kind of person did that? Surely, she must have been a tiny bit jealous when he got the Head of Key Stage 4 job. Or when he applied for the deputy head role, three years later. Or when, five years after that, Matthew applied for the Headship. Or when the board appointed Matthew CEO of the Academy Trust, on a salary that rivalled even Jeremy's. But as Jeremy watched her now, beavering through the cheese and crackers, he didn't see the monster he'd built up in his mind.

It was hard not to find some sort of appreciation for the person who'd first seen Matthew's potential, the young teacher who'd gone to his pupils' football games, caught them in tiny acts of kindness or diligence and praised them, called parents to pass on any last bit of good news to curry favour at home. She'd taken his husband and refined him until he was barely recognisable, given him authority and confidence. And it shouldn't matter if Jeremy couldn't give him those things himself.

In the lounge, Jeremy found himself on the edges of a conversation with some of the staff, all talking with their mouths full, none of them using napkins. He tried to remember their names. There was old Elizabeth Something, who had been Head ten years ago, and had retired after only two years in the role because of her 'health'. Along the corridors of the Academy, there was an uneasy whisper that Elizabeth's 'health' was a matter of *mental* health. Nobody asked her about it publicly but among a few in the staffroom there remained an air of fear and pity when she was discussed, as though she were an unexploded bomb or a learner driver who'd wandered onto the motorway.

There was the eagle-eyed head of HR, apparently still in the role, who certainly knew what had led Elizabeth to seek early retirement. At the moment she was talking about *Coronation Street* in Jeremy's house, but she looked like the sort to enjoy a good gossip given half the chance. In his mind, Jeremy groped for her name. Thea Somebody. That Nathan man was talking to a smattering of the other former students, some in their early twenties now, some older, some just out of sixth form; Matthew had insisted on teaching one class every single year as Head, right up until he got promoted again. How wonderful that Matthew had had such a positive impact on them that they would still, years later, read an email invitation in his name. And now they were in his home. Jeremy tapped his back pocket and the keys to the BMW jangled reassuringly.

A few of them, the former students, looked rather uncomfortable being here. A little wary, as though they had been lured here under false pretences. Jeremy watched them speak to one another in hushed tones, the children who had been allowed to stay up for their parents' party but who didn't know how to dance to the music. Too old to be the darling child on display, too young to interact with the retired and semi-retired crowd in which they found themselves. They sipped their wine cautiously, afraid to get drunk in front of people who had watched them grow up from behind a desk. Perhaps their clothes made them seem more awkward, too, the too-formal shirts and ankle-length skirts, chosen as if this were a job interview or a visit to grandmother's house. Which, Jeremy reflected, were probably the only other occasions on which people so young would ever meet people so… his and Matthew's age.

Someone turned to him, startling him out of his reverie. 'Sorry Jeremy, this must be boring for you.'

He became an actor again, made the usual polite noises, smiled.

'Your line of work must be much more interesting.' The man who was speaking was about ten years younger than Jeremy, and perhaps looking for a way out of a life of Saturday afternoons spent correcting spellings.

'I don't know about that,' said Jeremy. 'All jobs have their ups and downs, don't they?'

'What do you do?' said the man.

Jeremy mumbled something about tax law. The man nodded a little sadly, and the conversation went back to teaching, to what was said by whom in the all-staff meeting that morning. Something in Jeremy's mind sat down heavily as he realised that this was a world that simply did not stop. No matter who came or who left, no matter what had been achieved or sacrificed, there was always another cohort of children to be taught and fed and cared for, and none of them cared what happened outside their own tiny little worlds. And invariably the teachers were no better. He caught Mrs P's eye again from across the room. Was that her third glass, now? Did she even bring anything?

He went around the room with the wine, topping up glasses here and there, picking up bits of conversation as he went. Every so often he glimpsed the sausage rolls and had a thought, then set it aside. Maybe he and Matthew would have sex tonight. It'd been such a long time.

There was a gaggle of teachers in front of him, talking sceptically about the new skyscrapers in town. Jeremy forced himself to pour wine for them in no less generous quantities. He didn't particularly see where there was room for scepticism. The skyscrapers weren't some theory, or a figment of someone's imagination. And if investors were buying up the flats, so what? Renters needed landlords, and landlords need money just like everyone else. Wasn't this the city of the Industrial Revolution? When did everyone start getting so suspicious of the rich? His and Matthew's own investments were in one of the converted mills, where the modern Manchester had been born two hundred years ago. Beautiful flats, with so much exposed brick. Some people just couldn't control their jealousy. Jeremy smiled his bland, unconcerned smile and moved on, weaving through the crowd.

And there, like a sunset at the end of a long uphill walk, was Matthew himself. His husband, finally his again. Or he would be soon. Matthew was in the middle of a gaggle of slightly younger people. Jeremy recognised a couple of them as deputy heads, but Mrs P was in there too, and Nathan. Matthew, six foot three and still as handsome as he'd been in his thirties, made them all look up to him as they smiled and chattered on. He listened quietly and cheerfully - that was his way - and it gave him the appearance of being held aloft by them all. They were holding onto their wine glasses or their canapés, but it was hard not to see their hands all over him, owning him, claiming him.

But they'd have a good retirement. They'd both inherit soon. And the flats would make good money. One of them had a shower that needed fixing, as soon as enough rent revenue built up for it to be worthwhile. They'd get to it. And in the meantime, the income would help feather the nest.

As Jeremy got closer to Matthew, he began to hear them talking about the young man's job. He hoped to eavesdrop for a moment before being detected but Matthew spotted him and waved him into the conversation.

'There you are,' he said, kissing him on the cheek. 'Where've you been hiding?'

Jeremy shrugged. 'Around.' He said hello to Nathan again.

'This is my husband,' said Matthew.

'We met before,' said Jeremy.

'Oh. Did you know I taught Nathan when he was in year seven?' His glass was full, but he had a lot of a kind of energy.

'I actually remember you from before today,' said Nathan. He was looking at Jeremy. Jeremy glanced at Matthew with a hint of alarm.

'Mr Brown used to talk about you sometimes.'

'Call me Matthew, please. I think it's been long enough, now. And I'm not even a teacher anymore, after today. Haven't been for a while, really.'

'You used to talk about me, back then?' Jeremy did the maths in his head quickly. That was years before the repeal of Section 28. He couldn't think of anyone who'd ever lost their job for mentioning a same-sex partner in a school, but then he couldn't think of anyone who'd ever mentioned them in the first place.

'Never in class, never in front of everyone,' said Nathan. 'Just every now and then, with a few of us in Drama Club.'

'Oh,' said Jeremy. 'Even *I* know about Drama Club.' Truth be told, he mostly remembered Matthew working late, running rehearsals and performances. But every generation of kids had some variation of Drama Club, where the artsy ones and the loud ones, and the ones who liked dressing up in clothes not given for them, could get together under the guise (occasionally sincere) of actually wanting to spend time outside of lessons committing Shakespeare to memory.

'I might have been to one of your performances,' said Jeremy. 'What were you in?'

Matthew faltered for a second, but Nathan remembered.

He, after all, had only had one Mr Brown. 'It was *A Midsummer Night's Dream*,' he said.

His eyes widened. The tiny boy. Such a big voice. *I am that merry wanderer.* How had he not known, before?

'I remember,' he said. He would have said it even if he hadn't, but he did. It was the last play Matthew had directed as a classroom teacher, the last before he became Head of Department, after which he went from one play a year to one every three years. It was probably the play that convinced his Headteacher that he could handle responsibility, manage other staff effectively, think strategically. And afterwards, when Jeremy had told him it was a good production, he'd meant it. Matthew completely understood the magic of schools, the excitement of children on stage, knowing how to parlay that with music and costume, how to winnow it down to performance after hours spent cutting down the lines, explaining, rehearsing. Matthew had done that, and for this boy, who still remembered him now that he was a man.

'I played Puck,' said Nathan. Jeremy nodded, silently. In his mind, Nathan stepped out of one box, and into something else.

'And you were brilliant,' said Matthew. Nathan, who had clearly seen that Matthew did not remember this properly, blushed nevertheless. How old must Nathan be, now? 34? 35? And Matthew, giddy as he was on wine, was looking at him utterly steadily. He threaded his arm through his husband's and squeezed, but Matthew only shifted his weight slightly and smiled wider.

'You were such a good teacher,' said Nathan. 'We were all really sad when you stopped doing plays.'

'Well, you were a brilliant bunch. I was sad to give it up. But, there's no time. You'll see, when you get to my age.'

Nathan said that Matthew didn't look so old, and Jeremy felt a chill. They all sipped and smiled. Mrs P looked down at her shoes.

Matthew cleared his throat. 'Are you still in touch with any of the others, Nathan? Are they here?'

Nathan said they'd all gone in different directions after school. A couple of them had had children, not him though.

'And what are you doing these days?' said Jeremy. 'Are you still acting?'

'No time,' said Nathan. 'I'm a nurse.'

'What kind?' said Jeremy.

'I'm a theatre nurse.'

'So you've not left completely left the theatre,' said Matthew, and Jeremy laughed because there was something in their wedding vows about indulging your husband's terrible jokes, at least in public. He imagined Nathan's seemingly gentle spirit in a brightly lit room with some egomaniac surgeon who was breaking into an anaesthetised body, bone by bone. He wondered how Nathan liked such work, and if they made Nathan take out his eyebrow piercing in the operating theatre or if they didn't mind that sort of thing as long as nobody was awake to see it.

'And you're still living in Manchester?' Matthew said.

Nathan nodded. 'Where do young, cool people live, these days?' Jeremy asked.

'Town. One of those new ones.'

'Which one?' said Matthew.

Nathan named the building. For a fraction of a second, only long enough for Jeremy and Matthew to notice, and for each of them to notice that the other one had noticed, nobody said a word.

'That's a great building,' said Matthew, finally.

'Yeah. It's expensive.' He dropped his voice. 'It's kind of a sublet situation. One of the doctors at the hospital is letting us stay in her flat, me and a couple of friends.'

'Sounds quite crowded?' said Jeremy.

'She's in Australia,' said Nathan, laughing. 'Just for a year. But she's thinking about moving there.'

'And she's charging you rent?' said Jeremy.

'Jeremy!' said Matthew.

'It's fine,' said Jeremy. Mrs P inclined her head ever so slightly to the left.

'Just enough to cover what she's paying,' said Nathan.

'Do you like living there?' said Matthew. 'We used to live in the city centre. About a hundred years ago.'

'It's fine. It's in the centre of town, so I can walk to work and things, which is good. The shower's broken but my mate says she's afraid to tell the landlord in case he raises the rent.'

'I'm sure that wouldn't happen?' said Jeremy, quietly.

Nathan shrugged. 'Yeah, probably. The rent's so high as it is! My mate can only afford it because her family's loaded. I'm sharing with one of the other nurses or it'd still be too dear.'

Nathan laughed again, but it was like he was laughing into an empty space. Mrs P's eyes were on them all, flicking from husband to husband, and to the young man. And Jeremy knew she'd seen what he'd seen, that Matthew had changed hands so quickly that Jeremy hadn't even had time to reach out. He slid his arm out of Matthew's and his eyes wandered to the plate of sausage rolls. They were on the coffee table, still a few left. Maybe if he was quick –

Nathan said, 'So, Mr Brown –'

'Matthew, please,' said Matthew, cheerfully.

'Matthew,' nodded Nathan. 'You're still so young. What will you do, now you're retired?'

Soul Sisters

Reshma Ruia

SUMAN RENTS A ROOM on a quiet residential road. 45 Elm Street lies just beyond the clamour of Withington's shops and cafes. She quite likes being a lodger. It makes her feel young again, like her life is still waiting in the wings, a red carpet ready for her to walk on.

She works as a research assistant at the People's History Museum, a red brick and glass building that sits opposite the Civil Justice Centre in Spinningfields. Work is slow. Few people bother to go up to her cubicle where she maintains the records on the Suffragette movement and Emmeline Pankhurst's family life in Moss Side. Suman has plenty of time to read her novels, file her nails, or tweeze out the odd grey chin hair in a small magnifying mirror she hides in her desk drawer.

But on this particular day Suman has been busy fielding queries from an American PhD student who wants to know about Gandhi's role in the Lancashire cotton crisis. 'Well, we have no records on Gandhi… not sure if he even came to Manchester, but there is his statue in front of the cathedral if you're interested…' she hesitates. Her knowledge of Indian history is threadbare. She blames her mother for the gaps in her knowledge, for insisting that the best way of getting ahead in

England was to memorise the names of Henry VIII's six wives rather than learn about Gandhi. 'Gandhi won't put food on your plate in this country, but knowing who was beheaded first, Anne Boleyn or Catherine will impress your employers,' she'd advised.

Nipping out for a sandwich at lunch, Suman spots a man hunched over an ATM in the corner. It had to be Ashok. He has the same stooping shoulders and dark hair that turned henna red in the sun. She quite liked the chameleon colour change, said it made him look like a Bollywood hero. The man, his back still to her, stuffs the money in his front pocket and walks rapidly down a side street towards Victoria Station. She keeps up with him as far as Chetham's School of Music and watches him disappear down a set of steps. But can it be Ashok? He has moved down south, with a new woman, who now shared his life and heard him snore night after night.

Suman leaves work early, hurries home, changes into her grey velour tracksuit with its faded bleached back pocket and her fluffy slippers. Cuddling a bowl of Maggi chicken curry noodles, she slumps on the sofa and switches Netflix on. The blue television screen erupts in a blaze of colour and noise as a young woman bursts into song. She is gyrating her hips and swinging from a low-lying branch of a jacaranda tree. 'You come to me in the morning light and the silver of the evening moon. I see your face in the dewdrops and the ...'

'And the petals of the rose nodding in the breeze...' Suman finishes the line. Humming softly to herself she sinks back on the sofa, the TV remote nestling between her breasts. Who is she kidding, she could never sing like Mariam. Her voice was like a nightingale's and as for her size eight figure, that too was an unattainable dream. Suman closes her eyes and remembers. It was a warm July. A Friday. There was no rain for once and a crowd was sunbathing on the grass verge in front of the National Football Museum. The heat was like a razorblade slicing her skin. She was heading into the Arndale

Centre, to shop for some new summer sandals. The stores with their shiny glass windows and Ed Sheeran blaring on loop made her tired. Hot and sticky, she'd bought herself an ice cream cone. Peanut brittle and vanilla. A gaggle of schoolboys, satchels slapping against their thighs, snorted as they walked past her. 'Percy Piiiig…' Their voices still ring in her ear. At 42, she is still surprised by the careless cruelty of the human male.

Suman sighs, gets up and walks to the fridge. She is hungry. There is a Tupperware container with leftover chana and rice. She eats it cold, her back pressed against the thrumming front of the fridge. The spoon diving in and out of the container until it is empty. She thinks about calling her mother, telling her about how she'd almost seen Ashok and lost him. But she decides against it.

'Wake up, Suman. Stop daydreaming and hiding in them bloody films,' is what her mother will say.

★

Ashok walked out on her fortieth birthday, leaving her stranded at the George and Dragon in Altrincham. It was his favourite pub even though it was miles away from their home. 'See how the other half live,' he'd say, mouth hanging open, driving her past leafy, tree-lined avenues and houses tucked behind wrought iron gates. 'Nothing wrong with our Levy,' she'd shoot back. 'At least you step out the door and there's friendly faces asking how you are. You could die alone in these big houses and nobody would have a clue.' But Ashok had told her she lived a small life with no ambition. It was the World Cup quarter-final, England versus Sweden, and the pub was strung up with St George's flags. Men spilled onto the pavements gripping pints of lager. Women stood together, mouths knit in tense smiles. The pub had put up a giant screen in the car park and there was much female oohing over Gareth Southgate's blue waistcoat. Suman felt proud standing in the car park, staring at the screen, proud to be sharing her birthday with a national event.

Ashok told her to come inside.

'We'll miss the goals,' she complained as she followed him. All the tables were taken, but Ashok led her to the farthest one, the empty one near the ladies. Stupidly she thought he was going to give her a surprise gift. He knew she had her eyes on an Omega watch.

'The thing is, Suman,' Ashok said. 'I don't think I'm in love with you anymore.'

'Why?' she asked, thinking maybe it was to do with her love for Levenshulme and the Friday nights of fish and chips at Trawlers. Maybe she needed to think big. Talk of moving to one of those bright, spanking new tower blocks springing up like magic mushrooms in Deansgate Square and Castlefield.

His hands were flat on the pine table. She counted at least three water marks where his hands lay. She waited for his reply. He was studying his fingers as though they were arrows telling him which way to run.

A roar came from outside and Suman wasn't sure if the crowd was cheering for Ashok or Southgate.

She spent the rest of the afternoon sitting on the toilet, her head in her hands.

He had found someone else. It was as simple as that.

★

Ashok's departure disoriented her, unmoored her from her bearings and she began wandering the streets. Manchester had changed since she was young. Growing up in Burnage hadn't been easy, there were the strikes that filled the TV news bulletin night after night and gangs of youths with shaved heads who barged into her father's corner shop, demanding cigarettes and booze. Her mother began stockpiling tins of peach and Carnation condensed milk for emergencies. At one point, there was even talk of emigrating to Australia and yet, what she remembered most were summer days playing tag in the school playground and the 99 ice-cream cones she saved up her pocket money to buy. Her father's corner shop was gone, replaced by a fish and chip shop run by a friendly Turkish family who still remembered her parents. Gone were the empty warehouses with gaping broken windows and weed-infested footpaths that led to terraced houses and boarded-up shops. Lewis's had become Primark. There were slick department stores now and restaurants selling sushi and footballers wearing logos who purred along Princess Parkway in Lamborghinis and Ferraris. Sometimes she felt the city had grown taller and left her smaller. A bit like Ashok really. Her favourite area in this new version of the city was the Northern Quarter. She often stopped in front of Smithfield Market Hall or the Craft and Design Centre, staring through the Victorian glass-paned walls at the potters and painters busy at work. She could have been one of them, carefree, had life been different, less grey. Could have shopped for jeans at Afflecks while rummaging through vinyl records of Joy Division, instead of spending every weekend slumped in front of the telly, watching *Corrie* and reruns of the Take That concert at Etihad Stadium. While life moved on outside with bold, confident strokes.

The walks made her hungry and she'd pop into one of the artsy coffee shops, feeling timid and big and old. There were polished concrete floors and exposed pipes and moody-looking young men nursing soya milk lattes and vegan banana bread. The young, she thought, as she stirred the sugar in her cappuccino, what did they know of life. The bone-breaking heartache of it. What did they know of love, of having your insides scooped out and left like an unwanted gift by the roadside.

★

The room is dark. The film is over, silver-coloured credits roll against a flat black background. Suman switches channels. She needs noise and company. The news is on. Another bomb explosion in the Middle East or maybe it is Africa, she can't be sure. She stares at the images. It is like a video game, the streaks of light shooting against the dark of the sky. She hopes Mariam is okay, even though she knows Mariam lives in a gated compound in Mumbai, but one can never tell with actors. Their work can take them anywhere. Especially a woman like Mariam – at times Suman feels that every word she sings and every move she makes is dipped in blood.

Mariam's photo is taped on her wardrobe mirror. She'd found the photograph in an out-of-date issue of *Hello!* magazine at the dentists. The picture shows a woman with kohl-lined almond-shaped eyes. Her mouth is full and berry dark. Suman imagines it painted a crimson red. She walks up to the photo and strokes the faint lines running down the sides of the mouth. She has similar lines. Except they're much deeper. She runs a thumb down the sides of her nose. There they are, like a railway track going south.

'Do something Suman,' her mother said after Ashok's exit. 'You've got to find another man.'

And Suman did try. She went online and met Gary from Liverpool. She liked his brown eyes and suggested dinner at San Carlo, the posh Italian off Deansgate. He insisted on splitting the bill even though he drank most of the wine and wouldn't walk her to the bus stop. It was her cousin's turn next. She called Suman home for samosas and chai and introduced her to a young man from Delhi who was studying accountancy at Salford Uni. 'He'd like to stay on in this country,' the cousin said cryptically as the young man smiled and asked Suman about her hobbies.

Her mother suggested a makeover. 'Slap on some foundation, some lipstick, to make you look more bouncy, like the Kardashians.' So one afternoon Suman went to House of Fraser, pulled out Mariam's picture from her bag and said to the gum-chewing girl at the Bobbie Brown makeup counter: 'Make me like her.' But she came back home the same.

★

It began quietly, her love affair with Mariam Malik. Suman had gone to Withington Library one afternoon, her winter coat hiding her pyjamas. She stood bewildered in front of a shelf of books until a plump young woman with freckles on her nose came up to her, placed a hand on her shoulder, asked if she needed help.

'I am Agatha Kowalski, the new librarian,' the woman introduced herself.

'Do you have any instruction manuals on how to be happy? Some sort of do-it-yourself guide?' Suman asked, gulping hard and telling herself she was a grown-up woman who wasn't going to cry in front of strangers.

'Why would you need such a book, my dear?' Agatha's voice reminded Suman of cigarettes and black-and-white films.

'You're not an engine that needs fixing,' the woman continued. Suman's eyes had welled up at such unexpected kindness.

Agatha handed her a box of tissues.

'But then again, I may just have the right medicine for you.' She took hold of Suman's elbow, led her away from the bookshelves to a table in an alcove where stacks of DVDs glimmered in the winter light. 'These are Bollywood movies, they were donated by the old librarian, Mrs Patel. She picked up one DVD.

'*The Red Rose of October* – this was Mrs Patel's favourite. I've watched it too and I love the girl who does the dancing.' She screwed up her eyes, trying to read the names on the cover. 'Mariam Malik, yes that's her name. So beautiful, almost as beautiful as a fairytale.'

Suman was impressed. She was about to speak, but Agatha held up her hand. 'Wait, let me finish. This actress, this Mariam, you will like her, she is very sensitive. Every song she sings falls like a teardrop. She may be acting, but the pain she expresses is so real,' Agatha said, walking back briskly to the main counter.

Suman's eyes scanned the shelves for a book with a bold, chirpy cover, something like *How to Win Friends and Influence People*.

'You must watch this film.' Agatha's voice was firm.

'It's about a woman whose husband abandons her and goes off to war.' Agatha's eyes glinted behind her red-framed spectacles. 'That's men for you… forever chasing skirts and glory,' she added, handing Suman the DVD like a gift.

Suman wondered if Ashok was seeking glory and not a skirt when he walked out on her.

She watched the film in one sitting, rooting every step of the way for Mariam who defies tradition and becomes a successful corporate lawyer in New York.

'Life did not have to end just because your man walked out the door, the seasons still changed; the world still existed, she still had a brain and a healthy body.' (*The Red Rose of October*, 45 minutes from the start.)

She copied out the words in her notebook. And once finished, went back for some more. In six months, Suman had watched the library's entire collection of Mariam Malik's films.

She writes to Mariam's agent in Mumbai. The letters come back unanswered.

Suman files them carefully in chronological order.

★

'It won't be long before Mariam visits Manchester. I can feel it in my bones,' she confides in Agatha. The two women are close. Not friends exactly, but they sometimes share a chocolate brownie at one of those fancy cafes on Burton Road on Wednesdays when the library is closed.

'I'm sure I heard something about her writing a book

about her life… and going on a promotion tour. I think Mrs Patel mentioned it when she dropped in last week, but I could be mistaken,' Agatha replies and passes her, *The Tears for the Unknown*, Mariam's latest film.

'Keep up your spirits and stay clear of men. They ought to come with a health warning,' she says, squeezing Suman's arm.

Suman begins dreaming of Mariam. It's always the same dream, the two of them standing on a railway platform, Suman trying to reach her through the throng of commuters and Mariam walking ahead, always out of reach, looking back at her with a melancholic smile before boarding a train that whisks her far away.

A month later, Suman receives a telephone call. It's her brother.

'How's life, Suman?' he asks, his voice Cola Light. He doesn't care. She knows that. They are siblings, but their planets spin on different axes. And on her part she doesn't begrudge him his tinsel-happy life as a young man earning good money in London.

'The usual stuff,' she replies and waits.

'Are you sure you've not got your head buried in one of them… item girl's DVDs? What's her name – is it Monica?'

She hears his snigger down the telephone line.

'Mariam is a proper method actress. She almost had a place at RADA but couldn't afford the fees. She's not an ordinary girl just dancing around trees. She's much deeper than that.' Suman spells out the distinction carefully.

'Well, guess which deep actress is coming to Manchester,' he says. He's got Suman a ticket.

★

Suman rings in sick the next day and spends the day hunting for a new dress. She chooses a white frock printed with scarlet roses. On her way home from the Trafford Centre, she stops by the library and shows the dress to Agatha, lifting it out of its tissue wrapping like a magician pulling a rabbit out of a hat.

'Fit for a bride, not that you'd want to be repeating that mistake again,' Agatha says. 'I bet it cost a fortune.'

'I wanted the best,' Suman replies. 'How else will Mariam know it's me? I'm so happy I'll get to meet her at last.'

Agatha pats her hand. 'I'm so delighted for you. Let's celebrate and go to Rusholme for a curry.'

Lahore Kebab House is busy with students and intellectual types with beards and rucksacks, but they manage to find a table.

'Do you think you'll get to talk to Mariam? Isn't she like a celebrity person? How will you manage to get close?' Agatha asks, studying the laminated menu where each dish is accompanied by a bold colourful image.

'It will be a meeting of minds and soul. I can understand the pain behind her smile. Mariam will recognise me.' Suman's voice is firm even though her bottom lip quivers. 'I've waited all my life for her. I just didn't know it.'

★

Suman takes a cab to the city centre, making sure she reaches the Bridgewater Hall early. The doors are shut. She calls her brother to make sure he'd got the date right.

She imagines him at his desk: shoulders tense, face pushed against a computer screen.

'Why the hell did you turn up two hours before,' he laughs. 'Suman, stop being such a fangirl. Your ticket will be at the box office, panic not,' he says.

The day becomes a blur. She has a vague memory of crowds rushing past her, the orange marmalade of the sun spread thinly across the skyscrapers and cranes looming in the distance. At some point she must have been hungry, she remembers the chicken sandwich and lager at Rain Bar, her Cath Kidston tote crammed full of DVDs digging into her hip.

She is still early for the book launch but at least the doors are open. She studies the posters for upcoming piano recitals and concerts and uses the ladies to freshen up. The bookstall in the foyer is open now and she buys two copies of Mariam's memoir, orders a bottle of Shiraz and a packet of crisps at the bar, finds a quiet corner and begins to write in her notebook.

Question one for Mariam: 'Can I persuade you to shoot a film in Manchester? It has the best football teams in the world and some lovely museums. There is a nice Polish lady who works at my local library. She is a Bollywood fan too. Maybe I can invite you home and even cook for you. My ex-husband Ashok loved my cooking.'

Question two…

When she looks up, the bottle is empty and there is a queue outside the auditorium.

'Excuse me, excuse me… yes, family… friend of the actress… special reserved seat… special needs,' she shouts, pushing past people, breathless by the time she gets to her seat.

Her brother hasn't got her a front row ticket. But at least she has a clear, unrestricted view of the stage.

'Mariam's late. Isn't she? But then she is the star of the show.' She turns companionably to her neighbour, a bespectacled girl who scowls and mutters something inaudible.

★

Lights dim. Silence falls. A short-haired woman comes on the stage and takes the microphone. Suman wants the crowd to stop snivelling and shuffling and scratching. The woman taps on the mic. A crackle echoes throughout the room.

'Ladies and gentlemen welcome to an evening with Mariam Malik….' She clears her throat and explains that Mariam is in the middle of a global tour launching her new memoir. Angelina

Jolie has already snapped up the Netflix rights.

Suman edges forward in her seat, her knees squashed together.

'That's my girl,' she whispers. Her chest swells in pride. 'You show the world what we women are made of.'

And there she is, standing before her. Just for her. Mariam is petite with long brown hair. A turquoise necklace glints across her chest. The crowd are clapping but Suman stays silent. Her hands are shaking as she lifts her mobile and stands up. Murmurs of disapproval rise around her.

Mariam stares at her, framed in her mobile lens, her black hooded eyes – still and mysterious. The interviewer leaps up from her chair and grabs the mic.

'Please, no photographs. Mariam doesn't like the flash.'

The interview begins. Suman leans forward, tilts her head so she can listen clearly. She hears an American voice as Mariam reads aloud, flicking through the pages of her memoir, *Just An Ordinary Girl*.

'*I won't let you go to Mumbai and join the film industry. What will the world say? I shook my head. You are my brother, not my protector. I will dress and live how I want…*'

A woman starts clapping. Mariam raises a hand to silence her and continues. Suman is listening but the words spin inside her head. Mariam could be talking about her.

Looking around, she sees rapt faces. Hands move across paper, jotting down phrases. She too should be noting down Mariam's words, instead she is sweating and fidgeting. She blames the wine.

The reading finishes. Mariam closes her book and turns to the interviewer.

'I won't be taking any personal questions, so please don't ask me about my dog, my lover or the kind of flowers I like to smell. I'm more than happy to discuss my book and new film.'

The crowd titters. Suman's hand shoots up. The boy with

the roving mic walks towards her. His purple t-shirt says he is against dolphin fishing.

The insides of Suman's thighs stick together, damp with sweat. Her breath is sour. The moment to shine has arrived. She knows her question: 'Mariam, are you happy? Do you ever get homesick for love?'

But Mariam's American voice, her elegant clothes and the way she drapes herself over her chair makes her question sound foolish.

'Do you have a question?' The interviewer frowns. The mic hovers over Suman's face like a missile. She opens her mouth and sneezes.

Suman sits down, head bowed, ashamed. Her moment has passed. She listens to the others. There are questions about Mariam's acting. A man shyly admits he's doing his PhD research on her earlier films. Mariam nods and lifts her hand to cover a yawn.

★

It is over. People rush to form an orderly queue for the signing. Suman takes her place, her tote unzipped, full of DVDs and books waiting to be signed. It is clear to her that she needs to be alone with Mariam. Only then can they reveal their true vulnerable selves to each other.

The organiser hands out Post-it notes for the crowd to write out their names.

'Only one name, one book, no personal messages,' she announces. 'Mariam has a BBC interview right after. Please don't delay her.'

Suman writes her name and scribbles, 'Please meet me for a coffee, Mariam. We have so much pain in common. We are soul sisters.'

It takes her 25 minutes to reach the table where Mariam sits, pen poised.

Suman places the DVDs and the memoir in front of Mariam like corpses awaiting resurrection. Mariam signs the book, and pushes away the DVDs, including the note. Suman leans forward. 'I want you to read my message. Read it now please.' Mariam gives her a quick look and frowns.

'I don't have time. Can you see the queue?' She looks beyond Suman's shoulder.

'Next please.'

'There is no next please. You must promise to meet me. We have a lot of catching up to do. I've seen your films. You are a proper actress not just a dancing girl like my brother says… I can feel the pain behind your smile. Please meet me,' Suman pleads, still leaning on the table. Her bulk hides Mariam from the others. She must have raised her voice because the organiser is moving towards her.

'What is the problem?'

Suman smiles. She finds it funny, all this fuss over a simple message.

'I just want my soul sister to meet me,' she says. 'That's all. She knows me well.'

Mariam starts laughing. Her teeth crowding her mouth are small perfect pearls.

'What sisters… Do I even fucking know you?' She picks up Suman's note and tears it up.

Tiny pieces scatter on the table like snowdrift.

'Will you please move away madam? Otherwise I will have to call security.' The organiser's hand is on Suman's shoulder, nudging her out of the way.

*

The theatre empties. Suman waits by the door for Mariam to finish her BBC interview. A cleaner arrives, driving a little motorised hoover. Suman blocks his way, forcing him to stop.

'Are you all right, lady?'

112

'I just wanted to tell you that Mariam didn't mean to be rude. She was jetlagged and tired, that's all,' she says. Her eyes well up with tears. What will she tell Agatha?

She checks her watch. It is getting late. Time to head back into her sad, little life but then she sees Mariam, hurrying out of a side door, head bowed, deep in conversation with another woman. Maybe there is still a chance to connect, she thinks.

The women walk quickly towards the exit. Suman follows them. Couples walk past, heads lowered, hands entwined, the click of their heels like a wedding march.

A thousand stars scar the sky.

A road appears. The woman beside Mariam walks towards the tram stop. They shake hands and she disappears. Mariam is alone. She crosses the road near the Midland Hotel and looks around for a cab but none appear. The rain begins to fall and her long, dark hair sticks to her back like coils of rope. Suman would like to run her fingers through her hair. Maybe Mariam will gift her a lock, a little memento of their meeting. The hair will carry her scent. Suman stops, she feels lightheaded. Her mobile rings. It's Agatha. She lets it ring out.

Mariam is still walking and Suman steps up her pace, breathless by the time she catches up with her. But not quite. Mariam is still quicker. She crosses St Peter's Square, walks past the back of the Town Hall, crosses over and enters a white concrete industrial-looking building with heavy glass doors. Suman peers up to read the sign. All that grand talk about a movie deal and she is only staying in a three-star. She would have to tell Agatha about it. Why, if she had her way, she'd have booked Mariam a suite at The Lowry.

Suman walks into the hotel lobby, head bent, rummaging through her bag, as though looking for a room key. A group of American tourists are at the check-in desk, clutching brollies and iPads. She sidles up behind them, waiting her turn.

'I am here to meet Miss Mariam Malik... an interview. I'm from the Museum of...' She flashes her staff card at the receptionist who is jabbing the computer in front of him, while answering the phone. He is young with an anxious face and a badge that says 'Training'.

'Room forty-three.' He doesn't even look at her.

A Chinese couple are waiting for the lift. The girl is pale and slim, dressed in jeans and a t-shirt with little teddy bears embroidered in rhinestone.

'Your t-shirt is cute,' Suman tells the girl once they are inside the lift. The couple bow together, their heads almost touching.

'You must be newly married. Do you like Manchester? Have you been to Old Trafford? My ex-husband was a big Man U fan.' She hiccups and can smell the salt and vinegar crisps on her breath.

The lift doors open, her floor is there.

★

The night is dark and wet with rain. The streets empty of people. A cyclist in a high visibility yellow jacket pedals past the short overweight woman walking towards the Bridgewater Canal.

She meant no harm. If only the stupid girl hadn't tried to shout. If only she had sat quietly on the bed and listened to her story. But no, Mariam had to act funny. Why couldn't she stop screaming? The only way to keep her quiet was to put the pillow to her face. There was stillness then. And Suman could finally tell Mariam about Ashok. Tell her how much she loved her films and even though she sang and danced, she really was a method actress at heart.

Suman lingers on the towpath, watching the canal, sleek and shiny with nighttime lights.

The bag with the DVDs and the books cuts into her shoulder.

She opens her bag and lets them slip out into the waters below. They fall quietly, without making the slightest splash.

Cloaks

Yusra Warsama

THERE IS A CLOAK draped over the chair; the hospital gave it to my mum, that time she was ill. Her being in hospital… it wasn't the first time or the last.

At least there's a free little hospital gown this time. Something satisfying about a freebie I'll wear it to some Ancoats gathering full of 'gentrifiers' and make it look like some post-postmodern (shit) outfit. I'll slap a headscarf on too. No one cares much about much these days anyway. They'll other my body into another space. The gentrifiers will project unreconciled, ill-thought-out ideas of race and class and faith into the folds of the gown. The hijab would become 'kitsch' and we'd all listen to Aaliyah in the background. Coz everybody has access to the inner-city kid vibes from back in the day, they're on tap now. Coz inner city culture is mined, extracted, taken. Like blood diamonds. A blood drip-feed with no recompense. Estates never belong to those who've built memories on them. Land doesn't belong to those who've built homes on it. Everywhere in the world, it seems, we must move for either culture or riches to be extracted… But can't complain, can we… Cities are being handed over and colonised by the rich.

After the event, wearing the hospital gown, I'll cross Swan Street and head down Oldham Street. There'll be bottles being passed around. (RumBeat no less, because they all want some Caribbean South Manchester energy without getting too close). I'll tell them I don't drink as we walk to an after-party.

A gaggle… a troop, a clutch, a hoard… what do you call a group of posh kids and others trying to fit in?

They wonder how I have fun, if I don't drink or do drugs. Maybe I didn't get some 'how to access fun' memo. We'll get to the after-party: most of the females won't say hello till they're really drunk – something decided to make us enemies a long time before. Before we even get to offer one another a greeting, I'll think, they'll think, I'll bite. I never want them to be alarmed, yet somehow I alarm them. I try to resist being pushed into performing a pastiche of the identities they project onto me, just so that they can feel at ease. I don't want to be pinned to a wall. Why are some of these gentrifiers so dumb, when it comes to culture…? This is just a thought in my brain. About five seconds have passed.

The hospital gown looks like something beautiful. There is a golden afternoon light on the estate. From outside, it oozes across part of the fabric. It makes it look extraordinary, draped over the chair. People speak of the light in Rome, but they haven't seen the light at times in Moss Side. Each home will have the feeling of being its own hive, dipped in gold; each one a glorious salutation to the South Manc sun.

Honestly, the gown looks great. Maybe because it's free. I love a freebie. Can't lie about that.

My mum's voice is dancing. Engaged in conversation in the living room. I'm watching her and the chair with the gown from the doorway. She is beautiful.

'Make everyone a cup of tea, whoever's in the kitchen,' she chimes.

I take as many mugs as there are women in the living room and place a Yorkshire Gold in each one. I'm not making traditional tea. I feel like it will take forever and I feel a bit funny.

There are different places to belong and exist within –

there are options: I have where I come 'from', which is this city, and where I'm 'from from', where my parents hail from. The two spaces give me wide landscapes and earth to cultivate what I want. I can grind cardamoms and crush cinnamon to add in a pot with milk and loose leaves but I won't, because I want a Yorkshire Tea, golden brown, leaning into a strong builder's brew. Small options like these have been misconstrued into contradictions. The world where you're 'from from' seems to be under current investigation from the world you're just 'from'. These gaps, if not filled with sense, make lost boys and girls, I think. These boys and girls grow up with their tongues tied – words made thick and fat in their throats, they never expressed how they felt. Where they are 'from from' was used as a tool of shame. You see the landscapes in their mind become reduced to rubble, and it's affirmed when estates are separated by streets. There are streets where one type of people live and there are streets where another type of people live. Strategically placed by council planners.

They do it with the schools now too... When will our children ever get to truly meet, freely, properly, with all these invisible lines?

I'll walk into the council offices one day, maybe, and shout 'Hypocrisy' at the top of my voice.

I won't.

If I were to walk in, I can predict two reactions. First would be one of over-eagerness to connect, and the voice that greeted me would speak loud and slow. To make sure I 'understand'. The other would be a mixture of disdain, anger and disappointment. As if I've raped and pillaged the land of someone's ancestors. I might as well walk in with that hospital gown on, see if they even notice.

They know what they do in the council – the separation of people according to streets makes it hard for one to see the humanity of the other. Your neighbours should look like everyone, no? The young people carry the burden trying to reconcile 'home' and 'home home'. I wish they knew they didn't have to choose.

I cough, honey flies out of my mouth into my palm. I go to the kitchen sink and wash my hands. 'They poisoned the water for years in Moss Side, but not so much now that people with money live here' – the conversations you hear at bus stops give gold.

There is this sound of bones cracking.

My thoughts are in freight train mode. I must be looking for joy.

Something about observing ill health is boring. Predictable. There is a pain in not being able to help. Impotent before the one you love. Mother. Even late night prayers don't help, lamenting '*I'll* take some of the pain, give *me* some of the ill so she doesn't have to suffer, let *me* take all the darkness and only give that woman light.' We all know it doesn't work like that.

My aunt and my mother chat vigorously.

My feet seem to have a substance on the bottom of them. I lift my right foot up to look. There is a clear substance being secreted, the viscosity of hair gel. It makes it hard to walk. It feels like primary school glue. I walk to the doorway. One foot gets caught so I try to use the other to push against the doorframe. I lose my balance. I feel winded as my body whips back. My eyes close tightly bracing for inevitable impact. For my head to bounce off these imported Emirati tiles. My brain flashes the image of the shop that sells them on Great Western Street. And. And... it doesn't happen. I don't hurt myself. My feet are on the doorframe, suctioned, held, by the secreted substance and I am horizontal. I take a step. I walk up the jam of the door and back down again. I knock a few things off the side, feeling this new movement.

My feet come back down to the floor.

I'm sweating. I have several sensations all over my body, some new, some old. Is this fear or excitement?

I hear someone call me from the living room.

I open the hatch, between the kitchen and the living room.

'What have you been doing in there?' Aunty looks disgusted as she waits for me to reply.

She gives me strange look. It reminds me of the woman in Chorlton Library. This woman would look at me in a way that I could only deem a bit off, a bit funny. She would look at anyone of a similar hue to me in this funny way. Particularly women. I thought: Well, she has some enmity there. An enmity, which must be what's fuelling this look. This look she loves to give. Then I saw her one day in the coffee shop around the corner, with a young man of darker complexion, he must have been around nineteen... twenty. He was her son. It all made sense. Her look made sense. She was interested in the thing that her son has that she doesn't have. It explained those looks she had given when checking out a book for me.

Maybe she was trying to see him in women who looked like him. Or she was looking at these women to see if she could see his ancestors. She told me one day that he was her son, she told me how much she loved him, that it was just him and her. Maybe she lost her son's dad somewhere and part of her thinks he is stood behind us. Stood behind us women. Maybe she thinks if she looks at us intensely enough, her eyes will demand us to move, and as soon as we step to the left or the right...

He will reveal himself to her. The lost father.

But perhaps no one was ever hiding behind anyone. Her eyes just like to accuse me and others. Perhaps this is the silent invitation for me to offer some sort of apology. Perhaps it's because, despite the weight of looks and snide quiet comments, my shoulders remain back and high. Even though I just want to sleep. I should wear the hospital gown everywhere. I can then be identified firmly as off-key and be at peace. Maybe then I wouldn't have to wear the weariness of 'home'.

My eyes peel away from these images of the Chorlton lady and come back to my aunt in the living room.

'Why do you always seem to take so long just to make a simple cup of tea?' one of my older sisters asks from the next room.

The others call me – 'Come here' – in our ancient Cushite mother tongue. I work out I *can* walk if I move slowly and concentrate really hard.

I sneeze sugar from my nose. I wipe it with a kitchen towel from the counter that I grab as I head towards the living room. The journey ergonomically makes sense. They built this home when they still gave dignity to those in social housing.

I look at the room where these women sit. Members of my family. The light from outside is turning orange.

Another gown has appeared, it's draped over the same chair the hospital gown was. You see, let me give some context… Last night I commented on how beautiful one of my aunt's dresses was. An older cousin, who is currently staying in the spare room, overheard this compliment on her way to the kitchen. She backed it up and said Aunty So-and-So sells them,

'You want one? It's a butterfly dress.' Before I could even think to reply, a decision had been made by my mum and older cousin in silence and the dress-selling aunt had been summoned to the house.

I'd only came over to say hi to mum, now I was part of a whole thing.

I cough. No honey this time. It's a strange cough. My aunt, my mother and my older cousin break their conversation and look at me. They find the cough strange. The sound is strange.

'Are you sick?' my aunt asks.

'Drink some water,' says my cousin.

'This is because you never listened to me when you were younger,' states my mother.

'What? Because I'm coughing. It's because I once didn't listen to you?' They all look at me funny. I thought that's what I'd said. Instead a series of high pitch noises had come out.

I cough again. The sound is strange and vibrates inside me. I feel my skin flutter. They look at me. Four pairs of eyes, eight eyeballs, sixteen eyes dancing on each double heartbeat.

My aunt laughs. My mum looks at her to make sure she

isn't being malicious in her giddiness. Once she's convinced there's no malice, she adds a short burst of laughter to the room's sounds. Her beautiful face wrinkles for moment.

I cough again and again.

The laughter becomes nervous.

There is the sound of bones cracking again. This brings the laughter to a sudden halt.

After some time with them all staring at me, my eyes feel like they're beginning to poke out from their sockets. 'What are you doing? You're just doing it on purpose now,' my cousin says. They are all in agreement with this, and start up again with their laughter.

'She's always been the funny one out of all my children. Beautiful and funny.' She makes sure that this visiting, selling aunt accepts this as wonderful behaviour.

I try to say something. A strange sound comes out of my mouth. Stranger than the cough.

My skin feels warm, hushed from the sounds coming from my mouth. I don't look at them. I move as quick as I can back to the kitchen. Of course, I'm hardly fast with my sticky feet. As I turn, I feel their eyes on me. It feels like an age getting to the door. The silence of the women behind me thickens the air, married with the fear erupting in my belly at that very moment. I want to fold up into the earth beneath me and die. It feels like a shame that is on me.

One of my other sisters decides to come down from her bedroom. She passes me in the doorway, looks at the faces of the women and back to me.

'What are you doing, you absolute fucking weirdo?' she says. She pays me no more attention than that, giving the other women permission to look away and discuss some conflict that has begun at the behest of a gout-ridden dictator in a region near home.

I squeeze through the back door. My body has changed. I have transformed. The light is a darker orange and the sun is huge. It's beginning to dip behind the houses on Raby Street.

I move what must be wings that have emerged from my ribs, cracking. I lift up higher and higher into the sky. My mother's laughter erupts then slowly trickles away the higher I get.

There is nothing new under the sun; we all say that, don't we? Once you become aware of the unjust things hidden in plain sight, I think part of you yearns for the fate of Icarus.

I'm flying, I'm fucking flying and I can see all of Manchester. The land of Fred Dibnah, before the mill chimney's fell and the towers rose. I see Old Birley Street, once the last scrap of green in all of Hulme, where punks would have barbecues every summer. The buildings below look like cartoons, fake bits of cheap Lego. Structures that will no doubt be replaced once again in the coming century. The Junction Pub stares at the newbuilds, trying not to blink. Gentrifiers can't see memories. From up here, I realise they've never had the privilege to observe. Or maybe they choose not to. Poor areas are denied legacy, they're not allowed to form roots. It seems that only the 'haves' have a right to a permanent sense of home. You see, they can always *go* home. This is just a playground for them. But for us, it's our roots.

When you're this high you can see the layout of the city.

You can see that it's also made of invisible lines.

I try to hold on to some sort of infinite inner landscape, a place that can't be bought or scribbled on, or covered with buildings that look like cancerous sores.

I can see all of Manchester. I'm tempted to fly closer to the sun.

But I won't. This city is made of memories and my memories are made of it. The dissonance of it all flies with me, tucked into my butterfly-like shadow below. The Mothman is a Somali Manc girl who's become bored of it all. I won't fly too close to the sun. I'll bathe in its rays instead.

Ten-Two Forty-Four

Ian Carrington

HE TURNS UP LOOKING like a drowned rat or a soaked ferret or some other crappy animal dragged through piss that had no business being on my doorstep. The rain drips from his hands and his nose and whatever appendage that had not been chopped off by the torturing scum that had been holding him. For a moment, I say nothing despite all the things I had been planning on saying. Something about not trampling into the carpet or not sending me a postcard or some other witticism that, in truth, I am too afraid to say. Instead I just gawp at my brother so hard, it makes me want to laugh or cry or scream until my face bursts.

I am armed with a broom and a hardback dictionary. I stand down my weapons.

I find my voice. 'Ten-Two Forty-Four, you're damn well here,' I say, as if the government has conscripted me as senior minister of stating the blinking obvious. I call him by his government name because I know where he has been and I do not want that fight right now. I feint a hug but do not get too close. He smells of the city.

Ten-Two Forty-Four stumbles towards me, grabs me by the collar and says, 'Seven.'

He looks ready to collapse so I assume he has walked all the way from the labs. I steady him by the shoulders, partly because I do not want my long-lost brother splattering into a heap on my doorstep, and partly because I need to nudge the guy aside and take a look past him.

Since they pulled the plug in the putsch, all evenings are like this one is now. Virtual pitch black, the moonlight doing little to compensate for the no house lights, no street lights, no nothing lights. I listen for puddled footsteps in the street outside, or maybe a splash of tyres, the flap of raincoats. I detect nothing. He is alone. I think he is alone.

'In you come,' I say. More of a relieved rasp than an instruction.

My brother and his stupid name tramples into my house with all the subtlety of a hedge dragging itself through a hedge backwards. The candles lining my hallway flicker in protest.

'One six,' he says.

'They've turned you into a calculator.' I click the front door shut.

My kitchen doubles as my living room since the mould made its home as an unwanted lodger. The walls are a violent red; I had been meaning to get rid of the haemorrhage scarlet but what is the point anymore. My brother dumps his knapsack onto the kitchen table and then he is straight into the food cupboards. Trust him to remember where the food is kept. A jar of pickles in synthetic vinegar. Not interested. A packet of crackers with a complicated Swedish name. Not for him.

'Make yourself at home, then.'

He holds aloft an empty sauce bottle I probably should have thrown away.

'Seven six,' he says.

He is tearing a strip off me because of my dietary choices and he is yet to say a single non-numeric word. I have so many questions. How did he escape? How did they treat him? Did they stick spiders up his arse? I heard they stick spiders up arses. Now is not the time to ask.

'Do you want some cereal? I've got cereal.'

I pull out a chair. One of my wooden folding ones, only really used for getting to the high shelves. I gesture for him to sit, and he does not sit so much as slump with all the weight of the years upon him. His hair is in knots and his breathing sounds heavy. He looks like a pile of clothes rejected by a charity shop and left out by the bins for the homeless and for the crows.

'I have clothes you can have,' I say. 'Borrow.'

'Five,' he says.

I reach for a box of Standard Flakes. Brown package, brown logo. I scatter some into a bowl and make myself a bowl too although I am not hungry. There is no milk. My refrigerator lies dumped in a back alleyway somewhere. I add a splash of water to my flakes, from a bottle that has been sitting in the sink for two weeks. He frowns. No water for him.

'Here.'

I push the bowl in front of him and offer him a spoon. I close his fingers around the spoon, as if he has lost any kind of locomotion in his hand. Bit patronising.

'Six five four.' Obvious disapproval in this latest calculation. He yanks his hand back, lets off a harrumph with exactly the right amount of disdain, then spoons into the cereal. Takes a mouthful. Laboured crunches. It looks like he might vomit.

My flakes are soggy and I might as well be chewing wet leaves or something a stray cat has barfed up onto a pile of wet leaves. 'They taste like wood chips,' I say by way of an apology.

Conversation comes easy because I do the chatter and he says nothing, on account of the numerics. I reminisce about the neighbours. Angie and Kev, the couple that used to run the flower shop. We used to joke about it being a front for drug cartels. Shotguns snuggled in the long vases, Ten-Two Forty-Four had said once. The thought of anything so controversial happening in this cruddy village is stupid to me.

'Pretty sure they are working for the government now,' I say. 'Kev most certainly, such a dodgy lad.' I pick at my Flakes. I think I have found a hair.

I talk about the bookish guy with the one big shoe who went round with trays of religious texts. Two quid a tract. Or Red Ethel with the bloodshot eyes. A million years old and full of conspiratorial stories.

'She used to read our fortunes.'

He chews his horrible, dry food and glares at the back of the cereal box, at the grids of incomprehensible calorie information. I wonder if he can read, or if that function had been turned to soup.

A more interesting memory hits me. I reach into a high cupboard, where I keep all the plates I have never used. I drag out a handful of tatty newspapers. After the government scotched internet access, print papers were all the rage again, like Tamagotchi, beehive hair or smallpox.

'You won't remember these. They were… after you'd gone.'

'FOR MANCHESTER, FOR COUNTRY', says *The Manchester Guardian*. A page of blaring capital letters, yellow and black bee-themed flags bordering the text because the government's graphic design department had had a thousand strokes.

The second paper is plastered with recruitment advertisements for the new army. Photographs of starch-shirted do-gooders beaming at the camera. This first tranche of enlistees would bend over threeways for whoever barked the loudest orders. They got the good jobs, if you can call them that. Armament factories, clothing supplies, weapons refurb.

I spread the pages across the table. 'Get this. If you signed up to the army, you got coupons. Free shopping and everything.'

My brother paps the back of his spoon on a top corner of a front page, on a bright red blob emblazoned 'ONLY 30

PENCE'. He must think this is a bargain price, although if you pay 30p for a steaming pile of authoritarian horse puke, it is still 30p badly spent.

'Here. You'll like this one.'

I am not sure if he will like this one.

A headline reads 'LET'S HEAR IT FOR CYBER: TECHNOLOGY WILL ROOT OUT THE ENEMY'. Big block letters. Below this are paragraphs of jingoistic techno-babble that amount to little more than 'look at our labs, our labs are cool'. And set into this are pictures of smiling soldiers, some in uniform, some in white coats. In the bottom right corner, there is Ten-Two Forty-Four. His crooked smile; happy new recruit. Free meals and boarding.

'It's how I learned your new name,' I tell him.

My brother was taken in the third batch of recruitments, after things got heavy. After I had seen neighbours dragged by their necks into the conscription vans, I had kept my head low. I have no idea how my brother was taken because I was cowering behind a stack of laundry baskets.

'And now you're back.' My voice sounds hollow. The words hover in the air for a bit too long.

'Nine, four, five.' He barely looks at the paper, so I take this comment as a dismissal. Not bothered mate, you can shove that paper where the sun don't sprout. He pushes crumbs around his bowl.

This is hard work. I fold up the papers. I take our empty cereal bowls and clatter them into the sink. At least he has eaten the Standard Flakes which means he has an oesophagus which means he is my living human brother which means I can rule out him being replaced by a robot. Or a magic eight-ball.

The kitchen is starting to whiff. 'You stink of dead rats and shit,' I tell him. 'I'll get a flannel.'

It feels weird to see my brother so reduced. He was always the brash one, barrelling along the cobbles, owning the high street like he was lord mayor and may queen, while I cowered a safe distance behind him, stumbling into flower displays because I was reading a book while walking. Right now, he is counting individual noodles from a torn-open packet of One-Serve Content Meal. He is getting bits all over the floor.

Outside, the wind has picked up and there is a low hum in the air.

'Two,' says Ten-Two Forty-Four.

The rain has stopped. I sit on my doorstep, front door yawning open, and I look down into the miserable blackness of my cul-de-sac. My brother is in the bathroom washing off the stench of the city. The rat piss, the sewers, the chemicals, and whatever other toxic concoctions my overactive brain can invent on these long nights. He had better scrub up clean; this crap-box of a house is grimy enough.

Our estate is on a vast hill, a massive grassy boil on the arse of the countryside that overlooks the city. Down into the metropolis, I can see the yellow glow of the windows that lattice its colossal towers. Rising from the buildings are the illuminated erections of searchlights, which I suspect are nationalistic bravado rather than anything functional. The wind is in our favour tonight, so I listen to the city's faint mechanical symphony. Engine drones ebb and flow, sometimes giving way to the two-stroke rattle of something heavier, something military. For a moment, I hear an indistinct rhythm, probably a speaker system blaring motivational music. Every now and then, there is a sonorous boom, or perhaps it is a whoomph, and I imagine fields full of potholes and landmines scattered with dead birds and human limbs. The sound makes me queasy. One day the whole city will explode.

I lean back on my chair, which creaks in protest. Every now and then I devise an escape plan, in case they come for us with their probes and their clamps and their rusty thumbscrews. The options are binary. Further up into the hills, away from the city. Head for a forest or somewhere with cover. I do not think there is a river for miles, at least not a proper one. I could pick berries. Chase a rabbit. Become one of those foragers we used to watch when we had television. We would end up miserable and cold. Correct that. More miserable and cold. The other option is down into the city, right into the mouth of the fricking Godzilla. We would take our chances but at least we would have food and resources. We could get to the basements. Secret meetings. Find a ring of plucky resistance fighters, all of them skilled in code-breaking or electronics or kung fu. I'd work my way to the top. Become an anti-hero, get fit, grow a moustache. God, I would look great with a moustache.

I wake up with a jolt when Ten-Two Forty-Four turns on the hall light. The brightness of it punches me in the eyes. The street outside becomes emblazoned, every wet puddle illuminated in aggressive HD.

'Fuck's sake.'

For a moment, I want to strangle him, or at least have a very strong word. I slam the door shut and turn off the light. I hope nobody saw our instant beacon.

'Send up a flare, why don't you,' I say. 'Hey guys, we're here.'

Ten-Two Forty-Four is naked and shivering. The bath would have been freezing without heating. He pats himself with a towel patterned with palm trees. He is thinner than I remember.

'Seven one six seven. Four five. Five four.' A torrent of numbers. He sounds like he is admonishing himself.

I dig out an old jumper, and keks I used to go clubbing in, all splashed with designer jizz because clothing shops decided that looked cool. They fit him alright but he still looks bedraggled.

With him dressed and some sort of respectable, I empty his knapsack on the kitchen table and we take an inventory of the contents. A billycan. A dining fork, unwashed. Cruddy old clothes that may not be salvageable. Assorted tissues, which can bypass directly into recycling. A couple of leaflets destroyed by damp. A rain jacket that looks ripped beyond repair. And a ring-bound Haçienda: Gamma Phase manual, tatty and thumbed.

I reach for the manual.

'Six three.'

Ten-Two Forty-Four frowns again but it does not stop me. I open the manual. There are pages and pages of printed numbers, each one with the Haçienda logo, a screaming yellow face above a block capital H. Some of the numbers spill into equations. There are diagrams: flow charts and looping shapes. Some of them look like electrical circuits, mother boards or transistors or some crap like that. I did art history at Tameside College. This is not my expertise.

'Five four, two three two,' says Ten-Two Forty-Four, and he draws a finger down a spreadsheet of digits. The numbers are dense and in a stupid tiny font and they make my head hurt. His finger moves more slowly down the numbers than I feel comfortable with.

'Two,' he says again, this time with a half gasp.

I close his cult manual and vow never to open it again.

For supper, he picks a box of Protein Hoops. The logo is an infinity sign but constructed from maize. The box is almost empty, and there is barely enough for one. I look for something as a top-up. Canned raisins. Canned fruit cocktail. More canned raisins. I rummage for a knife so I can jab open a tin, but I change my mind.

'We need to go shopping while it's still dark,' I say. 'To get more food. I wasn't expecting company.'

We walk up the high street in a manner I would call brisk, or as brisk as we can be with a brother who keeps stopping at places he recognises to eulogise with random numbers. The old charity shop gets some proper fives and nines. It was once heaving with coiffured pensioners and is now burnt out into a blackened husk, silver coat rails scattered in rubble. A few doors down, he throws some numbers at the abandoned pub with the smashed windows where toothless shouty men once yelled karaoke until they vomited brown ale into the gutters. Its sign is half missing: THE SHAUN RYDER now reads THE UN RYD. When he reads the sign, he reads it in numbers. Some fours, a seven, the odd zero. I feel like a tour guide for a malfunctioning calculator and it is starting to get on my nerves.

I keep my ear out for any new sounds. I am well trained in this. Vehicles. Sirens. The chatter of army scouts out on a jolly from their mundane deployment in the city.

Nothing yet.

The shop is up the side of the old religious bookstore. The downstairs window is cluttered with dusty hardbacks declaring the apocalypse. *Sixty Ways The World Will End. God's Salvation For The Chosen Twelve Hundred.* We walk up the stairs, where two gawky teenage lads play sentry. I recognise them from the dodgy mobile phone stall that used to be on the market. One of them chews a pen, mangled with teeth marks, blue ink on his lips. I nod a hello while Ten-Two Forty-Four bleats them a three. They pay us little attention as we enter the old solicitor's office on the first floor, now the closest thing we have to an Aldi.

The makeshift store is illuminated by gas lanterns on window ledges, the windows themselves bin-bagged to keep the light from escaping. The moody flicker is surprisingly effective. Gaudy red discount banners hang from wonky ceiling tiles and cast sinister shadows on the walls.

We are the only customers. The shopkeeper is behind her counter staring at us. She is portly and permanently depressed. She wears the same green tank top that she has always worn.

'Shopping,' I say, as if she would assume we were there for some other activity like canoe lessons or astronaut school. I try to remember her name. Sue or Mary, that kind of flavour.

'Four,' says my brother in a way that is really not helping.

There is more metal shelving than product. A scattering of fresh produce on the left, packets and tins on the right. In the corner is an abandoned photocopier, no doubt once used by the advertising execs or brand managers or whatever hedge fund molesting corporate shills used to work in this space. My brother jabs its redundant buttons. He clearly does not want to be here, but there was no way I will let him out of my sight.

I squeeze a loaf of bread. It is as hard as a rock. The vegetable section is fine if you like turnips. No point in checking the freezer: that would have been unplugged a long time ago.

'No way she earns a packet from this place,' I say under my breath. 'She must do secret meetings or drugs or something.'

My brother is not listening. He inspects a stack of tins. Beans. Canned peas. Something called Family Nuggets In Nourishing Sauce. Several tins are without their labels.

'Five, five. Eight. One,' he says to himself.

I choose a bag of pasta, a squeezy bottle labelled Red Sauce, and a six-pack of toilet roll. A basketfull of other odds and sods. Ten-Two Forty-Four picks three of the blank tins. This strikes me as funny although I do not feel like laughing.

The only well-stocked section aside from the neolithic bread is the hardware. Shelf after shelf of crowbars, lead pipes, baseball bats acupunctured with nails, and something called EjacuBurn that is probably pepper spray. Pinned next to the display is a huge printed price list, each product itemised in bold black marker pen. I admire the nod to retail norms, but it seems obscene somehow. How do you value a crossbow that definitely looks homemade?

'We should go,' I say. I inspect a can of the pepper spray then put it back on the shelf.

I empty my basket on the counter. The shopkeeper has an

electric till, the kind that would go bleep if she had bothered to plug it in. She takes my coins with an all-encompassing sigh then scatters them into the open cash drawer. She never counts the money; none of this matters anymore. Next to the till is a plastic red charity box with labels peeled off, just like the tins.

'We should buy a can opener.'

'Seven. NINE. FOUR.' Ten-Two Forty-Four's voice sounds punctuated, every number a little more forced than the last. He stands next to the hardware with the crowbars and the dodgy baseball bats, just staring, firing out his numbers, like that's a normal fricking thing to do in a shop.

'He must want a crowbar or something,' I say to the shopkeeper, who is glaring at him like he is a dog that has curled a turd in the fruit and veg.

Ten-Two Forty-Four runs a finger down the list of prices, as if he is feeling every stroke of the marker pen. It is the same look I saw in the kitchen.

'Four. Six. SEVEN. Seven. SEVEN. SEVEN.'

'Come on, lad, let's get you home.' My levity sounds flat-footed amid this madness.

'Two. SEVEN. SEVEN.' Stroking the prices like he is trying to summon some sort of maths genie.

I wonder what the hell the scientists have done to his cranium to have him serenading signage like this. The shopkeeper is growling, her face as scrunched as the dehydrated cabbages on her veg shelves. She rubs her hands across her till keypad as if she is trying to wipe off the dirt of us. I cannot tell if her glare is confusion or anger.

I grab our bags and head to the exit, pulling Ten-Two Forty-Four behind me. I imagine the boys on the stairs blocking our exit, then me confronting them with… a pack of toilet rolls? I feel the weight of the ketchup bottle in the carrier bag.

Thwump. Thwump. Click. Thwump.

I look behind. The shopkeeper slams her price gun against

the counter surface. Bang, thwump, label after label, over and over again. She paints the counter in tiny stickers as if it is a terrible student art piece at a terrible student art show. She uses so much force, the charity box rattles in protest.

Thwump. She stares at Ten-Two Forty-Four, who declares a staccato 'Two!' Thwump. She slams the price gun again and my brother shouts a 'Five'. That price gun is going to break. THWUMP.

'Three. Eight. Nine. NINE,' says my brother.

We scurry down the stairs and I nearly break my neck because my brain has decided to forget how to walk. The market lads are gone which does not make me feel as relieved as I thought it would. As we stand outside on the pavement, my brother does not stop counting. All of the numbers. I want to shove the whole of our shopping into his mouth, just to silence the idiocy.

We pause a couple of streets away, outside the blackened shell of the charity shop. My vision swims and I somehow feel the heat of the long burned-out building. We take a moment with our shopping bags rustling and Ten-Two Forty-Four counting ten to the dozen.

Somewhere off to the right, I hear an engine. Quiet at first, and then the unmistakable glottal stop of a gear change. I hold my breath as if this will make my hearing ramp into pin-drop mode. The sound has the loose rattle of an old diesel machine. This is no neighbour. Someone is on a scout. My chest goes cold. We are only a handful of weed-patterned pavements away from the house, but it suddenly feels like cities away.

'One, one, nine, nine.'

I can hear the slam of the price gun, but I must be imagining it.

'This way,' I say, and we scoot back to the old pub, to hide in the shadows of The Un Ryd. My possessed lottery machine of a brother walks awkwardly, as if all his focus is going into his brain calculator. He bumps into a concrete bollard.

'Six. ONE. Six. Nine. NINE.'

The car park at the rear of the pub is bordered by gaudy fake bushes that, if I remember correctly, match the chintz of its interior. The imitation greenery is peppered with cigarette butts, moulded to the cheap plastic. The pub's back windows are scattered with motivational signs in novelty fonts. *You miss 100% of the shots you don't take... One day or day one: you choose.*

The engine still chugs away, and I have difficulty working out where it is coming from, on which street, from which direction.

We duck through the flower archway that leads into the centre of the car park. I somehow drop-kick a puddle and the water splashes up my leg.

'We might need to do a bigger shop some time,' I mumble, checking my brother is right behind me. 'There's a Mega Mall down the hill. It's closed, but there will be guys round the back selling stuff.'

The conversation feels useless, like a chocolate kilt at a morris dance in hell. But every time I speak, I swear his vocal rolodex spins a little slower.

'One,' says Ten-Two Forty-Four.

At the far end of the car park is a vehicle, but not the one we were expecting. A tractor is parked half onto a curb, wheels fully inflated and bodywork seemingly intact. It is cleaner than it should be, painted a strong and almost visceral red, with giant white number tens plastered onto its sides. A dump and run, perhaps. Stolen, or abandoned in a chase.

Once again, I start my mental coin toss between sneaking into the city or fleeing to the hills.

My brother the dickhead stands in front of the tractor, face made of storm clouds. He throws zeroes and twos at the tarmac.

'It's our ticket out of here, you idiot,' I say.

'One. One. Five. One.' He stamps his foot.

The jeep engine still circles our location. This corner of

the car park feels sheltered, the trees dripping from the rain. But this canopy is no help while we argue the toss over a tractor. No one has done cars outside of the city, not in the new days, so this tractor is gold dust.

'Three. Eight. Seven.' *Thwump.*

I see a compartment on the side of the tractor. I yank the handle and step backwards into a jacuzzi of stinking mud. I pull my foot out with a wet gloomph. My footprint looks like a bastardised eight. Screw this weather and screw the countryside.

'Nine. Zero.'

Nestled in the compartment is a toolbox. Rusted and mucky and containing much more useful things than my brother's rucksack. Screwdrivers, rolls of tape, elements of what I think might be a camping stove. It is hard to see in the dark. Under it, a dirty green tarpaulin, and next to that, something cylindrical. A torch, chunkier than the ones I have at home. If we cannot take the tractor, at least we can bolster supplies back at the house.

I take the bits of stove and try to drag out the tarpaulin. It does not budge.

'We've both got hands, you know.'

Ten-Two Forty-Four does not help. He looks at me and says 'Thwump'.

I think of the shopkeeper staring at us.

I tug at the tarpaulin but my head feels woozy and I stop almost immediately. For a moment I see my kitchen table and my brother's crap strewn all over it and suddenly I am back at the tractor in the mud and the cold. I swear that jeep is getting closer.

Ten-Two Forty-Four goes straight for the torch. And switches it on.

'Are you serious?'

Hedgerows burst into bright greenery and we can see tree branches interlacing for what feels like miles. I bat the torch out of his hands. The beam of light timbers to the floor, and the torch skitters beneath a hedge. I look at the light amid the undergrowth and I feel like screaming.

'Thwump,' says Ten-Two Forty-Four.

Under the tarpaulin is a folded sheet of waxy paper. It opens out into a map. For a moment I think I see the words 'ROOT OUT THE ENEMY' but I shake my head and the words are gone.

'Leave it,' I say and Ten-Two Forty-Four stops reaching for the discarded torch.

The top half of the map is the city. I can tell by the clusters of rectangles that represent the towers. Looming behemoths in real life but uninspired geometrics here. Like a line of number ones, arrogantly tall. The labs on the east side are illustrated with jagged lines, as if someone has lazily scrawled zeds or twos across the design. I remember this site from the before times: Hucknall Living, a mecca for digital influencers say the brochures, but boxy little prisons in real life. Sweeping across the lower part of the map are thick swirling lines, forming a barrier of eights from west to east. I picture the guards at the checkpoints, a line of sevens with guns strapped across their chests and– I look again. The map is all numbers. The map is just numbers.

My brother is mouthing something.

His face swims before my eyes and we are back in the house, me welcoming him at the door. He smells of sweat and he smells of the city. I am in the corner of the bathroom looking down on him and he is rising from the water and the water is red and he is dressed in torn noodle packet wrappers and the ripped shapes are all numbers and he is getting bits all over the floor.

The slam of a car door brings me back and I am leaning on the tractor and I say, 'We need to go shopping while it's still dark.'

My brother puts a hand on my shoulder and for the first time he smiles and he places a gold key into my hand.

He has stopped counting.

I want to hear his voice like it once was. Yelling at me for being a shrinking violet and why can't I just talk to people. Five. And I would shout back about him poncing about and getting all the attention. Hot heat rising up our throats. One. Wanting to shake the sense into each other. Three. I miss this about us. Eight. Stupid spats over how to cook breakfast. New Order versus Joy Division, and how we preferred James more. Seven.

We had a row in a vape eight shop once one one one. Two. An otherwise normal Saturday afternoon. Something about black four strawberry versus lemonade flavours six seven. The mental three picture fades. I feel so tired and goddamn I cannot remember why we are in this car park. Six.

Do you remember? I say but the words do not come out.

I am in the driver's seat of the tractor because I can tell by the red and it feels tall and four I have a key in my hand. Three. A golden eight key that reflects four the light, although I am not five sure where the seven light source is. The fob is leather ten ten and red and ten displays a number something-or-other one six four.

How do you start a tractor five? Stamp on all the pedals seven until it goes vroom? Show it pictures of farmers five five until it chugs with excitement. Tractors, two, the perverts of the countryside. I want to ask him about the spiders up arses. I place my hands at ten and two o'clock, at least I think those are the times.

Sometimes numbers spin around my head and I feel I will lose my balance. Sometimes I say numbers when I am not speaking and I do not know who is able to hear. Sometimes I see the numbers in the shadows of this countryside I am so desperate to escape. Thwump.

'Ten,' I say.

I am in the house but I am not in the house and my brother smiles and his face is ablaze with light. He is saying real words to me but I cannot hear and I do not want to hear and nine nine two four one four four five nine the jeep is right in front of us and its headlights blare and light becomes noise and the hum becomes the air and I want to shut the front door but there is no front door.

In the wall of headlights, silhouettes approach. Two skinny figures. One of them has a cigarette in their mouth, or maybe it is a pen. The other wields a baseball bat pitted with spikes of jagged metal.

A larger figure walks between them. Big woman. Army fatigues. She carries a gun, the kind that needs a strap. She reaches for my brother, who is now as stiff as cardboard, and places a hand over his face.

'Nine.' I know what is next.

I feel the dampness of the house. The musk. The chair pushing into me as I lean back. The creak of its legs. The sight of my brother raiding the cupboards. Stuff all over the kitchen table. The smell of the mud. The smell of him. The red walls. The crunch of cereal. We are outside the flower shop. We are outside the charity shop. Thwunp. It is ablaze. I feel the sharp slice of broken glass. The pub window. Above it, the missing letters on the pub sign reform into numbers. Five for an S. Three for an E. Thwunp.

'Nine,' I say again and I know I am lost. I look at my brother but he is gone. I feel like I will burst. I turn the key in the ignition.

One six. Seven. Seven zero two three. Four. Nine four two. Five nine eight eight six one seven eight five. One three three four two seven six seven five one six five four eight nine eight one two five three nine four seven eight nine one one two three three three six two six seven nine one five four three eight five five four seven six four one two eight three five nine eight nine ninefive four three two six three zero ten eight five one twoseven four zero two six two five five one nine four seven twonine one fiveonefour eight five threefourfivefour nineeightoneoneone

Occupy Manctopia

Mish Green

WE WAIT TILL DUSK to pull up in my car, take the spot near the bushes, watch. Rain melts the streetlights down the windscreen.

'Ready,' Benny says. Nerve up.

This woman stands at the door, smoking, her face a series of pastel-lit slides as she scrolls her phone, and when she finishes and throws her cig butt out into the night, I get out of the car, shake my umbrella open and jog over. I jam my foot in as it closes behind her and she disappears into the lift.

I keep the umbrella low and turn to the office on my left. Like I remembered, the lock is a five-pin tumbler. Same as the one at work. I pull out the keyring of tools and my pulse bangs in my ears as I rake the lock. What if this doesn't work, what if someone comes in right now and -

- soft click, the fifth pin. I lean gently on the handle. I'm in.

★

Two months before this: I woke every day confused, car seat all the way back, windows streaming condensation. My new home, post-Lianne. I mostly parked in the little roads off Newton Street. Not too far from work, but less trouble, fewer eyes.

Then the dry cough set in. I started sleeping in the office above the Oldham Street shop, just till the cough settled. Everyone else was working from home by then, so what did it matter?

Now it's routine. Each night I turn the main lights off at 8pm to maintain the illusion of emptiness, and each morning after a bird bath in the tiny sink I go downstairs and move the donation bags from the doorway. The shop's shut for the foreseeable, but that doesn't stop people piling bags of old clothes beneath the Sudan Appeal poster in the window.

I'm just the administrator, so the odd jobs fall to me. My job's mostly online now anyway, even without the apocalypse, so nothing much changes. I end each day with a Pot Noodle on the office sofa, scrolling Li's socials, her new life: I press on the bruise. Ache.

I call the housing office and estate agents every day. 'Last name, date of birth.' Always a statement, never a question. Proof of citizenship, proof of income, postcodes of five previous landlords. I should mention that I'm working. They treat me better when they hear that.

'Download our app,' the voice says. 'The traffic lights show where you are in the queue for each property you're bidding on – green means top five, yellow is top ten, and then there's red.'

I cried the first time I scrolled through the list: red red red.

Now it's routine, like washing my pants in the sink then drying them on the radiator by the photocopier. The admin of transient life. I make the phone calls first thing, keep my voice light: '...maybe something in a lower price bracket? No, I'm not on benefits –' Betrayal. Putting on what Mum calls her phone voice, knocking the Scots edges off so you don't sound common. 'OK, no problem.'

I open the app and it takes forever to load. Tell myself I'm doing it for someone else, which sort of helps, until I'm stopped by a dropdown list that wants to know my current

142

situation. What's the difference between no fixed abode and homeless, between sleeping in a car and sleeping rough? There's prison, there's hospital, there's living in a boat and squatting and staying with friends and I don't know, I don't know how to do this. Bed and breakfast? Hotel room? How much will that cost?

I see a one-bed in Wythenshawe and I bid on it even though it's red, hundreds ahead of me, no chance. Still.

Go outside, look at the sky, forget. Walk to the end of Oldham Street and then across the big junction and zigzag right into the stark silence of Ancoats. I breathe in hard to suck back the tears that are threatening to spill, and when I look down again I see this ghostly young guy bounding towards me with both arms in the air, huge grin on his face. Scruffy dark hair against his collar, head to toe in grey.

'Red!' he shouts to me.

It takes a second, then finally: 'Benny?'

A rush of relief at the friendly face. We first met years ago outside Piccadilly Station where he sold poems to the commuters. I even bought a few, and kept one in my wallet – something about the Mariana Trench, deeper than deep.

We step towards one another to hug, then remember. He offers a fist bump instead.

'You wanna go get some coffee?' he says.

'Yeah, yeah, of course! There's a place round the corner that's still doing take out.'

We've barely set off when I tell him about the breakup, Li's new girlfriend, the lot.

'I'm sorry,' he says eventually. 'That's rough.'

We get coffees and start a slow walk. Great cliffs of red brick mills rise on either side, CCTV on each corner and door. The edges of the stone glow green with algae but there's nothing else growing here, not even a rogue patch of moss.

'What do you wish you'd known when you first got...' I search for the right word. '...here?'

He sucks in air like he's about to tell me how much it'll all cost. 'How little sleep I'd get. Forever knackered.'

We turn at the car park and the street gets shabby quick, more like it used to be. Tags and broken glass, feral grass. Some guy off his face, muttering into a sleeve.

'Like camping without the nature or relaxation.' Benny continues. I remember the tent in the underpass last winter. Someone said an old woman was living there.

'And you find your weak spots. The ones you didn't know. Stomach, skin, feet.' He pulls a manic grin and points to his ramshackle smile. 'That's mine. Stress and a shit diet. Gym membership used to be a good investment – showers, lockers and that, somewhere to get warm – but the pandemic saw to that.'

We walk past a bundle of sleeping bags twisted at the foot of a service door. A leg stretches out, and Benny cocks his chin at the bundle. He lowers his voice. 'And you don't tell none of them that you're homeless, none.'

The stop sign at the corner rattles as we approach.

'I've started bidding on council flats,' I say.

'Used to be able to go down the housing office once a week,' he says, 'and mither 'em till they put you in a tower block just for some peace. Squeaky wheel and all that. S'how I got the flat for me and Mum, before she– still took ages but not like now where it's all online, traffic lights and points like a grim gameshow that lasts eight years and ends in a studio in Harpurhey, *if* you're lucky.'

We turn back onto the main road as a bus bounces over a pothole, blows dry leaves across our feet in a gust of air.

1-bed multi-storey flat, Newton Heath
No dogs
7th floor
Over 60s only
RED LIGHT

I see Benny every few days now. It's just easy, little brother vibes. We walk a slow route round the inner ring road today and I trail my finger across the railings outside Band on the Wall, feel the beat of a gig from a few years back. Tanya Tagaq, screaming for her ancestors.

'You're gonna need a project.' He picks a bit of baccy off his tongue, twists the end of the rollie, jams it between his lips. 'Hold onto your mentality,' he says from the side of his mouth, 'cuz it's way too easy to lose that out here.'

'I guess...' I try to remember the last time I got lost in drawing.

'I've got one for you.' His lighter flares. 'How's this? You know the old council blocks on Chester Road roundabout next to them new builds on the canal? Stake 'em out. I bet you could get a flat in one of them. You've got more chance, being a woman, and no one with kids'll want in there after Grenfell, even on the ground floor.'

'They're still living in bedsits and hostels.' I read about it the other day when I was trying to find out what happens while you wait for a flat. Years. Years is what happens.

'Aye, who gives a fuck about poor people and immigrants, right?' He shouts up at the empty office blocks, and then points defiantly at the glass tower ahead of us. 'We should just take it. That's how them lot took the old Cornerhouse most of last year. It's still legal if it's commercial property. As long as you can hold the doors there's nowt they can do but take the slow road through the courts.'

Chester Road roundabout, near my first Mancunian home. I wonder if the neon shop is still there, and the pizza place that sells everything two-for-one.

'What I'd do is watch 'em each night, keep a record of which flats light up once it gets dark. Few weeks. Then you'll know which ones are empty, what might be coming up.' I knit my eyebrows. 'Summat to do while you wait. Occupy your mind.' He pulls hard on the roll-up and blows above us so that the plume trails us like a steam train. 'A project.'

1-bed flat in low block
Thorncombe Road, Moss Side
RED LIGHT

That night, after work, I take Benny's advice, park up across from one of the old council blocks and watch the lights flick on and off. I sketch it in the back of my work's diary, crosshatching each window as it winks light at the night. Calm satisfaction when, at 10.32pm, the lights are briefly symmetrical.

The heat of the day still hangs about so I drive to the other side of the dual carriageway for the 24-hour cornershop. One last orange juice before sleep, maybe some food, although I'm not hungry. Just want the comfort.

Not long ago, this side of the road was all scrubland and the deconsecrated church. Great bushes of mugwort cracking concrete in the empty lot and the old Victorian warehouses full of artists' studios behind panes of milky glass. Now it's a mix of money and tension, same one that defines this city. Boarded-up railway arches and rough-as-arse chippy one block down from a gin bar selling twelve quid cocktails in jam jars. Maybe it started when they converted the church. Probably before.

The ground floor of this building ahead of me has the hollow look of an architectural drawing, clear view straight through to the other side. Every so often, someone walks by. I count them, marking the edge of my page for each. Blue lights sweep the ground floor unit as a police car turns off the roundabout, and for a moment the inside is lit up – blank walls.

Later, I wake with a start to a red-faced man barking at my window, ugly laugh as he slaps the roof, and when I recoil to the passenger seat, he howls with his two mates. They stumble on, stopping to swipe in at one of the electric gates.

1-bed flat in low block
Belle Vue Street,
Gorton West
RED LIGHT

Over the next few nights I start fleshing out the drawings in the back of my diary. All these skyscrapers springing up on the scrubland south of the city centre. They look mostly empty. I don't get it. Who's buying them? All I can find online is a load of bland corporate titles, strings of uninspired Latin names, one owned by the next: Holdings, Limited, PLC. They're registered to addresses across the globe, so I mark them on the world map at the front of my diary. Kuwait, Cayman Islands, British Virgin Islands.

I follow one company and draw it on to the map like it's a puzzle. Line of ownership between the dots. Kuwait to UAE. UAE to Guernsey, Guernsey to London. An arterial flow of money from untaxed investment funds to the edge of Hulme and this building in front of me.

We should just take it. I think of Benny shouting up at the office blocks the other day, and now I feel it in my chest like a drumbeat.

1-bed flat in low block, Clayton
55+
No Pets
RED LIGHT

The next day I find him outside the cafe and when he asks how I slept, instead of detailing the blossoming aches and fitful sleep, I start in on the idea that arrived in the night.

'Woah woah, slow down. What office? You mean your work?' I shake my head, barely take a breath.

147

'No. This empty building, one of the new builds by St George's – the ground floor's an office with nothing in it, so it's fair game, right? Section sixteen?' He just stares at me. 'The squatting law?' I grab my diary from my bag and start leafing to the sketches in the back.

'Section six,' he replies.

'Right. Six. It's commercial, so we could...'

'What's this "we"?'

'You and me.' I show him the first sketch. 'This is one of the old blocks. Lights on, people living here, right?' I flip over the page. 'Then over the road.' I point to the windows marked with an X for lights off. Only one light. 'They're practically empty.' I flip to the map. 'I've worked it out. Most of this block is owned by a company here,' I point to UAE, 'that owns a company here,' and I trace it to Kuwait. 'But the wealth really starts over here in Sudan, the dictatorship and the war in Darfur. It's all in a report from this researcher in Sheffield.'

'Look, I'm glad you've found a project but –'

'I've been reading about it. The regime in Sudan got overthrown by student protests a few years back but basically the same people are still in power, same company connections. They amassed all this wealth from quietly selling off oilfield rights and investments in airlines, all to fund the regime's war in Darfur. And the money the investment company made from *selling* that oil...,' I retrace the path to UAE, Guernsey, UK, 'arrives here in Manchester. Buys these fucking flats. Uses them as storage for war profits.' I hold my finger down on the drawing of the empty new block. 'Mate. Manchester's a genocide bank. The money that made people homeless in Darfur came from the same company that's now paying for these tower blocks here, driving up rents and keeping people homeless in Manchester. It's fucking–' What word can hold this? The horrifying link.

When I eventually speak again, my voice is lower. 'What if we squat the office on the ground floor? Occupy it.' He laughs, throws his cup in the bin and keeps walking.

End of the block and he doesn't slow down. 'Benny.' No response. I jog over till we're shoulder to shoulder.

He turns. 'It comes so casual to you. Like what is that?' Heat floods my face. He twists the end of a rollie, his eyes everywhere but my face. I open my mouth to reply and he speaks again: 'What, you've been to a couple squat parties back in the day so you know what it's about? Fucking *nothing* like what I've had to do. See that?' He pulls up his sleeve to a mess of scars. 'That's my last stint in the nick after a place in Cheetham Hill got pulled apart by Manchester's finest.'

'I'm sorry. I just...' He lets out a long sigh and I don't speak.

The traffic navigates slowly round an ice cream van that's broken down in the outside lane, still wailing its playground tune despite the fact we're in November.

Benny's staring up at the glass cliff ahead of us. 'Look,' he says. 'I know you mean well. But you can't fix this. It's not just me and the other scruffs out here, but all them that are stuck with their kids in stinking damp rooms for years, invisible, like fuckin'...' he chokes. 'Kicked out their only home because their mam died so what's left for them anyway.'

He lights the cig with a shaky hand, pulls on it, and keeps his gaze low. 'It's a full-time job not sinking,' he says, and instinctively I reach out and hook my arm round his.

We lean into one another. 'What if, this time,' I say slowly, 'everyone's watching. What if you're not alone.'

With our shoulders touching, the ice cream van finally dies. We stand together for a long time and he breathes in deep and when he speaks again, his voice is steadier.

1-bed flat in low block
Manilla Walk, Beswick
RED LIGHT

'It's an unusual time to be looking,' I say, and the agent cuts me off.

'No, not at all. We're seeing lots of clients converting traditional rental properties to HMOs, for example – *big* growth there - and the international market's always lively. Is your client interested in new builds or conversion?'

'Bit of both,' I say, and she seems happy with this.

'Diverse, that's great,' she says. 'So: how about tomorrow afternoon, two o'clock?'

After we hang up, I google HMO. Housing of Multiple Occupation. Bedsits, in other words. Small and cheap, full of people like me. Worse off than me. She was right: it's a growing market, especially for big Victorian houses that can be chopped into tiny Victorian rooms and rented at a premium to the council as temporary accommodation in the middle of a housing crisis.

The next day I arrive in full business drag: face of daytime makeup, charity shop suit. I hold my hand out to her and she pulls back.

'Someone said we should do elbow bumps instead of handshakes but that seems a bit–' She twirls her fingers in the air and I think she grimaces behind her mask. 'Anyway,' she says, and ushers me into the foyer, reeling off a list of amenities.

'Cameras at the door, inside and out, and one in each lift. Twenty-four hour off-site monitoring at a nearby suite, key codes and alarms, very secure, no issues at all since the first domestic tenant moved in.' She is keen to reassure, create distance from the council estate across the road.

She takes me round a two-bed two-bath and I make use of the silence, pivot on my heel to take it all in. 'How many like this?'

'Twenty-one two-beds and eleven singles,' she says, and hands me a brochure with her business card clipped to the top.

'I'll need to speak to my client,' I tell her, and then we

head back towards the canal-side entrance. As we cross to the main door, I slowly turn to the door of the office suite. She follows my gaze. 'The commercial unit...' I say, and she jumps in, her eyes brightening.

'Shall we take a look?' she asks.

2 bed Flat in low block
Woodstock Road, Moston
RED LIGHT

Benny's humming while I flip to the drawings in the back of my diary. 'Here,' I point. 'Midsize office unit. Door here,' I say, 'cameras here. None in the unit. There's twenty-four-seven monitoring in the entrance so we'd have to assume we're being watched when we...'

'Oh right,' he says. 'B&E's part of my skill set is it?'

'Sorry, I–'

'I'm winding you up. Anyway you're the Weegie,' he says with a grin. Cheeky fucker. 'So what's the plan?'

I take a long breath. 'You know how everyone got into hobbies in the first lockdown–'

'Yep, the Sourdough Life.'

'Right, well my g–' I catch myself. 'My ex gave me a lock picking set. Transparent plastic thing so you can see inside the barrel, so I started with that and I've now worked up to practising on the doors at work.'

'OK, say we do get in. Then what?' he asks.

'We go public is what. The shell corporations, the ghost towers. How many people are homeless in the middle of a lockdown. This whole circus.' He doesn't say anything, and I start to falter. 'Maybe a journalist at the *Evening News*, or. I dunno, I–'

Benny suddenly slaps his leg. 'Did I show you my socials?' He pulls out his phone and opens them one by one: '*Word on the Street*. I started it during first lockdown. Bits of poetry and that, videos, and a Patreon. It's not loads at the minute but a couple of people have signed up to give me a few quid a month, and every video gets me a few more people.'

It hits me. 'We livestream.'

'Yes, that's what I'm saying! "Live from Manchester's Blood Towers: Occupy Manctopia."' He spreads his hands like a marquee. 'What do you think?'

★

The morning after our break-in I wake up all sweaty on an unfamiliar floor. Sunlight from a window. 'Morning, chuck.' I come to and realise where I am, feel the jolt of adrenaline. What if someone sees us here, what if –

'It's fenced off at the back,' he says, reading my mind. 'No one can see in. We're fine.' He blows the steam off the top of his tea.

I make some shitty coffee with the travel kettle I brought and then put my suit back on and brush my hair. Scroll through my phone.

'Hello, I manage a commercial unit on Deansgate Wharf for Shadrack & Duxbury, the letting agents. I need to get the locks changed, ASAP. We've had to let someone go, and we need to make sure we're secure before the tenant moves in next week.'

A few questions later and I'm booked in for 1pm. I feel for the estate agent's card in my jacket pocket, and then check that the power banks I charged up at work are ready for tonight's launch.

One o'clock arrives and with it the locksmith. Benny hides in the toilet and I straighten my jacket before I answer the door. 'Here's my card, in case you need to follow up.' I hold it out and he doesn't even look at it.

He works fast, gets it done in ten minutes, and as he packs up I say, 'Can you Bluetooth me your bank details? It'll take weeks if we have to go through Finance.' We stand there fiddling with our phones for a moment, and I empty half my account. Fuck it. It's done, paid, and I'm thanking him, standing there with my customer service smile until he's back in his van and pulling away.

'We're clear!' Benny leaps out of the loo and we jump into a hug. Fuck it, I don't care. Hold on tight. 'I guess we're a bubble now?' he says as he cracks a can and hands it to me. 'Right, let's get that legal statement up on the door.'

THIS IS A NON-RESIDENTIAL BUILDING
Section 144, LASPO does NOT apply

This is NOT a "residential building" within the meaning of section 144, Legal Aid, Sentencing and Punishment of Offenders Act 2012 because it was NOT designed or adapted, before the time of our entry, for use as a place to live (ss (3)(b)).

The provisions of section 144 are therefore NOT APPLICABLE to this building or to our occupation of it.

Part II, Criminal Law Act 1977
(As amended by Criminal Justice and Public Order Act, 1994)
DOES APPLY

LEGAL WARNING
TAKE NOTICE
THAT we occupy this property and at all times there is at least one person in occupation.

THAT any entry or attempt to enter into these premises without our permission is therefore a criminal offence as any one of us who is in physical possession is opposed to such entry without our permission.

THAT if you attempt to enter by violence or by threatening violence we will prosecute you. You may receive a sentence of up to six months' imprisonment and/or a fine of up to £5,000.

THAT if you want to get us out you will have to issue a claim for possession in the
County Court or in the High Court.

The Occupiers

'People of the Republic of Mancunia! We come to you today from an undisclosed location in the centre of Manchester's hot property belt.' Three people are watching. My face looks weird. My turn.

'Over the last ten years, countless new units of housing have been built in central Manchester: but for who? Uh whom?'

My tongue sticks to the roof of my mouth. I cling to my notes.

'A recent study of twenty-five thousand new homes built in Manchester and Salford showed that only *five* met the government's definition of affordable, which is defined as costing eighty percent or less of the average market rate in rent or sale. –' Eight people are watching. 'The council's own–' I swallow hard, 'statistics–'

Benny taps my knee with his knuckle and leans towards the camera. 'I know, right? Makes my head spin. You can read the Housing Legislation Act online if you like – two hundred and seventy-seven pages.' He mimes his head exploding. There he is: natural storyteller. 'It's a massive tangle of information. Look, she drew it all out–' he grabs my spider diagram from the folder in front of us and holds it up. 'We're gonna untangle this, one thread at a time, because you need to know it. If you've been watching over the last decade you've seen the change. Skyline full of cranes. Every doorway with a sleeping bag and someone who looks like me.' He stops for a beat. 'And that's just what you can see.'

As he speaks, my heart rate evens out, my breathing slows.

Seventeen people. 'I'm living in my car.' The words are out before I realise it. 'And my work's office. I work for a charity and–' I shift. 'During the first lockdown I was home like you might be right now, learning a new hobby–'

'And how's that going?' Benny asks.

A laugh bursts through. 'Better than knitting.' 23 people. 'Back then we were told that rough sleepers were being housed in the empty hotels.'

'Yeah, that's true actually,' Benny says. 'I spent most of April in the Ibis watching *Say Yes to the Dress.* Proper good sleeps, but still eating shite because a kettle's not a kitchen.'

'Right. But what about May? June?' I ask.

'That's when they started to quietly turf some of us out.'

'So here we are. In this empty office in an almost empty block of new flats. Built in 2018 and mostly owned by an overseas company. Get this: each *parking space* sold for fifteen K. That's more than I've ever made in a year. Serious.'

Benny whistles. 'Nice little earner.'

I point up above us. 'These homes have no people and these people,' I gesture to Benny and myself, 'have no homes.' I look around us at the white walls. Feel the momentum build. 'That's what we wanna talk about. And to understand it, we need to follow the money: Guernsey, Kuwait, Sudan.' I hold the map up to the camera, trace the lines with my finger. 'It connects back here, to this city, these flats. These blood towers.' Suddenly self-conscious, I run dry.

Benny steps in: 'This has been the first instalment of a guerrilla expose of Manchester's housing crisis. Follow, like this post, and to the twenty-nine of you watching this right now: share it. We'll be back soon. Laters.'

He hits stop. We both exhale, and then we laugh big belly-deep laughs that hurt the way we need to hurt, that ache with relief.

After that first livestream, we get into a rhythm: one of us goes for supplies during the day, to stretch the legs, get some air, while the other one reads through the folders and decides what we're gonna talk about that night. We gather more and more followers. More comments, which brings more bots of course, and trolls. We keep going.

I'm still working in the office three days a week, combining it with a food run before the evening's broadcast.

'People of the Republic of Mancunia: I'm Word on the Street–'

'– and I'm Some Homeless Lass–'

'– and today we're gonna talk about squatting during the pandemic–'

'– rough sleeping during the pandemic–'

'– evictions during–'

'– healthcare–'

'– poverty during the pandemic'

'You know how time feels completely messed up now? Like March 2020 was twelve weeks long? That's a trauma thing. Time gets busted. One day is a week and a week's a month. That's homeless time. Street time.'

We keep each broadcast under five minutes, and we start asking questions:

'What's the worst place you've ever lived?'

People are watching. And commenting: the bad landlords, the harassment, the mould, the rats.

We go live every night at 8pm, once people have had their tea.

'There are fourteen thousand, nine hundred and twenty-seven homeless families across Greater Manchester tonight. And that *doesn't* include people like me, the so-called hidden homeless who aren't in the system. The invisible majority.' I glance through the window to my car. 'There are twelve-thousand, six hundred and seven empty homes in all. *Five* out of every six families could be housed tomorrow. Tomorrow!'

I let it hang for a moment. 'This city that we're so damn

quick to mythologise as radical, rebellious – this great city of Manchester is working as it has always worked. For the mill owner and property speculator and landlord and the rich. For blood-soaked "investors".

'I know you've heard that thing about how you're three paycheques away from homelessness yourself, but have you *felt* it? In your bones? Not as a theory but tomorrow morning. Start counting the friends who might let you stay on their couch for more than a week. Start working it out. How long do you think you've got?

'One breakup or layoff that you can't quite muscle through and you're here, with us. You are us. Already. One accident. One fuck up.'

'One virus.'

I pause. Grip my keys. I hold one up to the camera: the key to the flat.

'Take this away and what have you got?' I let it drop to the bottom of the ring, then hold up my car key. 'And this one?' Hold it for a moment. Say nothing. Let it drop. I look down the camera lens, imagine Li looking back at me. The rage. The pain.

Benny looks down for a moment and then ends the stream. I lean back and breathe out, hard.

Next morning we wake to a tapping at the window. Taped to the outside: a chain with a key on it, with a note, facing in:

> *This is the key to my old life. Locks changed.*
> *Don't stop.*

We take photos of the key and the note before opening the window and bringing them in. That night we share it on the livestream, and when we get up the following morning there are five more.

People start coming down each day. Randoms, people we don't know standing outside on the little patch of lawn, masked up and holding homemade signs:

Homes not Hedge Funds
Occupy Manctopia

A little kid on their dad's shoulders holding up a drawing, that classic five year old rendition of home: little grids for windows and a triangle roof.

The bailiffs arrive and they try to chase off the crowd but with everyone masked and in pairs or alone, they can't stop it. It's like catching water in a sieve.

Benny's on the laptop, scrolling our feeds. 'Let's post this as an update,' he says. 'The unfolding drama of – hang on.'

'What?'

'Last night's video.' He studies the screen for a moment, scrolls. 'Shit.'

'What?'

'It's blowing up, we're going viral!' I rush to his side. 'It got shared on the housing justice page, *The Big Issue*, this huge Gen Z TikToker – ' we scan down the list of names, of shares and likes '– *The Guardian*.' He opens their article.

'"Manchester's Blood Towers – the council's shame". It's going mental – look!' he scrolls down. 'Blood Towers is trending.' Hundreds of comments, thousands of hits.

Our nightly broadcasts now have thousands of viewers, thousands of comments and shares. The protestors and protectors are joined by bailiffs who try the office handle periodically, banging on the door and shouting through closed windows.

Just after lunch, Benny taps me on the shoulder and points to the parking lot. A woman holding her mobile against the window: a number.

I hesitate for a second and then pull out my phone, dial, put it on speaker.

We lock eyes as she answers: 'Channel 4 News. Your supporters have just delivered nine wheelbarrows full of keys to the front steps of the Town Hall – fourteen-thousand, nine hundred and twenty, as many keys as there are empty homes across Greater Manchester – in protest at the housing crisis. What do you have to say about that?'

I stammer, and Benny speaks: 'Tune in tonight to find out.'

As we start the livestream that night, the locksmith's van pulls into the parking lot. The bailiffs are at the door.

Now, it has to be now. I hold a gold key up to the camera. 'This is the flat I lost in the divorce.' I let the key drop.

Benny: 'And this one is for the two-year temporary B&B.' He lets go.

Line by line, we speak what we've spent all afternoon writing: 'These are for the couch surfers (one, two, three) and the storage unit and this one got thrown out when she came out.

'This one time-shares a single bed with two guys from back home, shift work even when he's sleeping. This one breathes black mould all night and this key trades sex for a bed.

'This one got bedroom taxed and this one's been found fit for work, long Covid and nil points awarded by PIP on the basis that he can make himself a cup of tea.

'This one sleeps outside the Tesco Metro, the key to his old life still round his neck, gets called a "hero" once a year on Remembrance Sunday and "scum" the rest, and this one grew up round here, can't pay the rent and they don't give mortgages to dinner ladies do they.

'And then there's these - people, situations, trying to manage, humiliation clinging to them like the smell of a damp flat and we're told that she's got a bad attitude, and he's an anomaly, that they aren't representative, that these metastasising colonies of bedsits and empty towers are progress: business is booming in the City of Cranes.'

Time was you could get a flat in this town on a part-time wage. Small and rough, but you could do it. It's why so many artists, the music – that's how that happened.

This key used to open a house that's now an estate agent's window and this one opens the past like a wound that never really healed right. It still hurts on cold nights. That's why we're sitting in an empty room in an empty building in the middle of a second lockdown talking to you about homes.'

We fall silent for a moment, stare down the camera as the comments and reactions flood in. The locksmith's drill bites the door.

'You ready for this?' Benny asks me. I look round: *What do I need?* For a moment it feels like the last time I left in an instant, losing everything I knew. I look up to see Benny's smile as the drill breaks through. Warm eyes, home.

I smile, then turn to the camera:

'We all deserve better. Occupy Manctopia,' I say to our city, and as the door handle falls and hits the carpet I let the stream run, record what happens next.

About the Authors

Stockport-raised **Tom Benn** is an author, screenwriter and academic. His fourth novel, *Oxblood* (Bloomsbury), was longlisted for the Gordon Burn Prize, the CWA's Gold Dagger for Best Crime Novel of the Year, and won the Sunday Times Charlotte Aitken Young Writer of the Year Award.

Salford-born **David Constantine** has published several volumes of poetry with Bloodaxe (including *Collected Poems* (2004), *Nine Fathom Deep* (2009), *Elder* (2014) and *Belongings*(2020)), as well as two novels (most recently *The Life-Writer* with Comma) and six collections of short fiction: *Back at the Spike* (1994), *Under the Dam* (2005), *The Shieling* (2009), *Tea at the Midland* (2012), *The Dressing-Up Box* (2019), *Rivers of the Unspoilt World* (2022) and *In Another County: Selected Stories* (2015). He is the winner of the Frank O'Connor International Short Story Award (2013) and the BBC National Short Story Award (2010). He is also a translator of Hölderlin, Brecht, Goethe, Kleist, Michaux and Jaccottet. He is the winner of the Queen's Medal for Poetry 2020.

Ian Carrington is a Manchester writer who, as 'Fat Roland', has enjoyed a long performance career including a solo show commissioned by The Lowry, 'Seven Inch', which contained over 200 self-scrawled cartoon props. He co-compered live literature night Bad Language, twice voted the UK's best regular spoken word event. For over 100 issues, he has written a music column for *Electronic Sound* magazine alongside feature interviews. At Easter 2023, Ian experienced a stroke: 'Ten-Two Forty-Four' was written during recovery amid post-stroke eyesight defects and hallucinations caused by his mangled brain.

Born and raised in Salford, **Shelagh Delaney** (1938-2011) was a dramatist and screenwriter. She is best known for *A Taste of Honey,* for which she won the Foyle's New Play Award and the New York Drama Critics' Circle Award. She wrote the screenplay for the film version with Tony Richardson and was awarded the British Film Academy Award and the Robert Flaherty Award. Her other screenplays include *The White Bus* and *Charlie Bubbles,* for which she won the Writers' Guild Award. She also wrote for television and radio and published a collection of short stories, *Sweetly Sings the Donkey.*

Mike Duff is an author and poet from Collyhurst. His poem, 'In the Rain', won the Poem for Manchester competition in 2004. His novels include *Low Life* (2000) and *The Hat Check Boy* (2007), both published by Crocus Books.

Mish Green is a Manchester-based writer working in poetry, short fiction, and hybrid non-fiction. They are currently writing a collection of sea-level stories based on Hayling Island, following their critically acclaimed debut, *Jebel Marra* (Comma Press, 2015). Their work often explores the overlaps of class, gender, disability and migration, and they recently created a spoken word audio tapestry for *Disbelief Disregard*, a University of Liverpool research project about chronic exhaustion and social care.

Peter Kalu is a poet, fiction writer and playwright. He cut his teeth as a member of Manchester's Moss Side Write black writers workshop and has had nine novels, two film scripts and three theatre plays produced to date. He gained his PhD in creative writing at Lancaster University in 2019. He has a first degree in Law from Leeds University, studied software engineering at Salford University, and Languages at Heriot Watt University. In 2018, he was writer in residence at the University of West Indies (Trinidad campus). For many years he ran a carnival band called Moko Jumbi (Ghosts of the Gods) which took to the streets at Manchester Caribbean Carnival on three-feet-high stilts.

Okechukwu Nzelu is a Manchester-based writer. In 2015 he was the recipient of a Northern Writers' Award from New Writing North. In 2020, his debut novel, *The Private Joys of Nnenna Maloney* (Dialogue Books/Little, Brown), won a Betty Trask Award and was shortlisted for the Betty Trask Prize, the Desmond Elliott Prize, and the Polari First Book Prize. His second novel, *Here Again Now* (Dialogue Books), was published in 2022. He is a lecturer in creative writing at Lancaster University.

A graduate of the University of Manchester and MMU, **Sophie Parkes** is currently studying for a PhD in creative writing and Folklore at Sheffield Hallam University, for which she won a Vice Chancellor's Scholarship. She is an Associate Lecturer in creative writing at Sheffield Hallam and Leeds Arts Universities, and founded the community writing group, Mossley Writers. Her historical novel, *Out of Human Sight,* was shortlisted for the NorthBound Book Award at the 2021 Northern Writers' Awards and was published by Northodox Press in 2023.

Reshma Ruia is a Manchester-based writer. She has written two novels, *Something Black in the Lentil Soup*, and *Still Lives*, winner of the 2023 Diverse Book Readers' Choice Award and longlisted for the 2023 Peoples Book Award. She has published a poetry collection, *A Dinner Party in the Home Counties*, and a short story collection, *Mrs Pinto Drives to Happiness*. Reshma's work has appeared in anthologies and journals, and she has been commissioned by the BBC, University of Cumbria and Manchester Literature Festival. She is the co-founder of The Whole Kahani – a writers' collective of British South Asian writers.

Brontë Schiltz is a journalist with *The Big Issue* and *Big Issue North*, a freelance contributor to *Horrified Magazine*, and a PhD candidate with the Manchester Centre for Gothic Studies at Manchester Metropolitan University, where she researches the Televisual Gothic (horror on and about TV). She is a writer of short stories, flash fiction, creative non-fiction, poetry and theatre, and her work has featured in publications including *Lotus-eater* magazine, *Olney Magazine, The First Line* and *Hungry Ghost Magazine*. She has also appeared on podcasts including *The Ghost Story Book Club, Victorian Legacies, BERGCAST* and *Chronicles of the Quarter Life*.

Stockport-born **David Sue** is a writer, journalist and editor of Comma's Reading the City series. He began his career in the music industry, working alongside Tony Wilson at the influential In The City music conference. As an arts journalist, he has written for a variety of publications including the *Guardian, NME, The Big Issue in the North, Time Out* and the *Manchester Evening News*.

Yusra Warsama is a Manchester-based artist, writer, actress and theatre-maker. As an actress, her credits include the Royal Exchange's *Nora: A Doll's House*, TV dramas like *Castle Rock* and *Deliver Me*, and films such as *The Last Days on Mars* (2013). Her writing includes poetry and plays such as *Of All The Beautiful Things In The World*.